Raping the Gods

Brian Whitney

A Strawberry Book
www.strawberrybooks.com

Strawberry Books is a publishing house that thrills, delights and informs our
readers with high-quality e-books, physical books and online content.
Please check out our website and follow us on Twitter:

@thrillsdelights

To my buddy Tim, who came up with the name.

He who wishes to be obeyed must know how to command.

Niccolo Machiavelli

CHAPTER ONE

I didn't feel like talking to him, but I needed a drink, and he was buying. I only had about 15 bucks on me, which in this place wasn't as bad as it sounds. They pour heavy here and the drinks are cheap. Still, I had to make it through the night on the little cash I had, and Brad said he was going to buy me a drink, so the dance began.

I hadn't seen him in quite a long time, he was a friend of a friend kind of dude. He went to law school with a guy that I used to hang out with back in the day. I think he found me amusing. A lot of these types did. I said things they wouldn't say, I did things they wouldn't do. Through me they could live a life that they imagined they wanted, but knew they didn't.

He was a lawyer now, he had some cash and he was drunk. I was a writer, I was broke as a joke and I wasn't nearly drunk enough. Therefore we had an arrangement for the next few hours. He would buy me drinks while I gave him the feeling that tonight he had really experienced something. That he had a big night out. He already was making comments about how much he would like to bang some of the chicks that walked past us. I would have joined in and said something similar but most of them hated me.

There are positive and negatives to being a bar regular. The positives are the fact that everyone knows you. The negatives are the fact that everyone knows you. There are five women in here that I know. I have lied to all of them at least once, fucked three of them, and stolen from one of them. If I wasn't so hammered I would feel a little uncomfortable.

Any true drunk knows the genesis of the bar regular.

Step 1. People don't know you. You come in often despite that. You start buying drinks for others, tipping well, saying funny things.

Step 2. You now get said hello to by all the staff and regulars, you get a free drink here and there. People know you so it is easier to bum smokes and get laid. You say things and people laugh. Sometimes you even leave on your tab, and come in the next night to clear it up. They all trust you, it's fine.

Step 3. You have bummed too many smokes and have fucked too many people. You now take the fact that you used to tip well as a reason to tip badly. The staff and regulars still say hi, but it is forced. You say things and you are ignored, albeit in a polite way. The last time you left on your tab you didn't come back in for a week to pay because you were broke.

Step 4. You find a new bar.

Brad sent me a message on Facebook a month or so ago and

wanted to get a drink. To him, this is his night. I can imagine him planning this for weeks. Asking his wife if it is okay, making sure things are all smoothed out. I know his wife too, she isn't all that bad in general, but I know right now she is sitting at home hating the fact that Brad is out with me.

Pretty much everyone I used to hang out with is married now, and most of them have kids. I mean I still hang out with people but they keep changing. Over time they all get married, or they go to AA. I am the last man standing, the guy that all of these dubs call for their big night out. I am more than happy to oblige, I get nervous if I sit at home too long, and lately I have been so broke that I have been home more than I would like.

So we drink and we tell each other stories. Brad is an associate at his firm now, he has a little boat, and he has a new house. He has three kids – they already had twins, but that wasn't enough so then they had another baby. Who does that? He has two dogs. He has a cat. He tells me stories about his boat, about how he should be making more money at the firm, how those fuckers are greedy, how he works hard but they don't give him enough money.

I have stories too. I've been divorced twice. I don't own anything other than my clothes. I left everything I had at my second wife's house and have been bouncing around ever since. A lot of my stories are the type that you can't tell to a guy like Brad, so I make shit up instead.

I don't have a bank account. I bounced checks with my last two banks so they closed the accounts. I have like 600 bucks in a sock drawer. I live with my girlfriend, but I don't like her. Well I do like her, but not that much. I haven't had a real job since I quit working at the homeless shelter two years ago. Even though I quit, sometimes it is like I am still there. I see the homeless dudes all around town, and they all remember me.

I saw Wyatt sitting in a doorway right before I came in here. I fucking hated Wyatt. He was a drunk and his pants always had shit in them. He would yell at me and call me a cunt. He would take out his dick and piss on the floor in the soup kitchen.

When I first started at the shelter, they gave me Wyatt to work with. This chick that was his caseworker was leaving and he needed a new one. The girl I took over for had these really wild eyes and an awesome ass. She is pregnant now, she got laid and then dumped by a wannabe rock star. She is the type of chick that is all into yoga and says "Namaste" all the time, but in reality you know she is going to wind up with a drunk guy that slaps her around.

I remember her saying over and over again shit like "Oh you're going to have fun with him" in a sarcastic manner. As a matter of fact pretty much everyone that I worked with said something like that when it came to me working with Wyatt. It was like they all knew I had herpes but I didn't know it yet.

They gave me Wyatt mostly because I was weird. They gave me all the freaks. They would say things like "I really think that you would work well with Wyatt." What they meant was "no one else can deal with this piece of shit," but no one would say that.

We were social workers, you know? We cared. We smiled and we would give the homeless people fist bumps when they walked past us in the shelter. We had meetings and we talked about our clients and we always made just the right type of concerned faces.

Me and a couple other guys I worked with wondered at times what the fuck we were doing. Like if we were to just stop feeding these dudes, and giving them places to sleep then they would rise up and take over the city. Then shit would just be natural law and people would have to do something about what was going on. Instead we just gave them chicken fingers to eat and a cot to sleep on, and everything was okay. Like we were zookeepers, feeding the animals and keeping them in cages.

This one guy I worked with named Sean used to talk about that stuff a lot. He said he was an anarchist. He was a married anarchist who drove a Chevy Cavalier to work every day. He wanted to go out and get drunk at night, but he knew his wife would get mad so he didn't. He was that kind of anarchist.

I hated being there at first. I was there for the same reason anyone was. I fucked up along the way. I had some sort of career at some point, and I fucked it up so I ended up working at the shelter. I cared what happened to these guys but I sure as fuck knew I wasn't going to be able to do anything about it. So my role was basically to give out cigs and shoot the shit with people. I was good at both of these things.

Anyway, back to Wyatt. So he would come in and fall over and yell at people and call us all cunts and fall down and shit his pants.

I remember this one time at the soup kitchen. People volunteered there, it was a big thing, it made them feel special. They would come in and they would bring their kids. Or sometimes it was a church group or an insurance company or some shit. This time it was a field hockey team, lots of young smiling blondes with taut, yet round asses.

They would all come in and they would look around and they would smile and serve meals and then they would go home and tell people how they volunteered at the shelter. They would tell their boyfriends, and their moms, and when they applied to college it would be on their application. Yay.

So this one time Wyatt sits down in the dining room and he is way too fucked up to stand up, and swearing and being a dick and all that. So I don't care, but this guy I am working with kicks him out. So as he leaves he gets in my face and balls up his little fists and yells at me and calls me a cunt and threatens to kick the shit out of me. He has food in his beard, it appears to be some spaghetti.

So I kick him out. I fucking kick him out and I try really hard not to punch him. I succeed somehow, just for today I let him live. He slumped down outside, next to the door. One of the field hockey players looks at me as she sees him there. She gets down on one knee, and she wipes his beard off. She gets really close too, and as she does it she looks up at me, but she speaks to him and she says, "There you go, I know it's so hard and all you need is a little help and the people that are here to help you aren't doing it."

And I say, "that was nice of you to get that spaghetti sauce but I think what is really making him cranky is all that shit in his pants. You might want to get that while you are at it."

I hated that job. I started banging the boss. I also got her weed because she didn't know where to get any. For some reason I told everyone that I worked with about it. That was a mistake. Sort of. It got her fired and got me in a position to quit and collect unemployment. I know this sounds bad. I've grown a lot since then.

So now I write books. After I got divorced the last time I wrote this book that I thought was this overwrought view into my soul. I sent it out to hundreds of different publishers. An erotica publisher picked it up. My pain is another guy's orgasm, I suppose.

From that I got a deal to write another book, and then I got a ghostwriting deal with a porn star named Summer Starr. The book is going to be out in a few months. I got an advance and soon I will start making a little money off of it. I do mean a little. None of this pays bills. I shovel snow part time for 15 bucks an hour in the winter to get by. Sometimes I get a little royalty check here and there. I wrote a book and put it up on Kindle about how to run a successful escort service. That gets me money for smokes.

I am currently shopping a book I wrote with a chick from New Hampshire that has lupus. She just gave me a couple hundred bucks to do a sample chapter. The chapter is beyond horrible. She calls the book "Caffeinated Smile." I told her I thought it was a good idea. It isn't.

From this ghostwriting gig with Summer I got a few more. I got a book deal with a semi-famous cartoonist. He is a guy in his 50's that used to hang out at this very bar. He drank nothing but Bushmills. Even when he was broke he would act like you were being an asshole if you wanted to buy him a drink that was cheaper than Bushmills.

We got an advance, but he lost his apartment because he couldn't pay the rent and has been living with his mom out of town ever since. He hasn't done shit on the book. He sits in his room at his mom's house drinking Bushmills and tries to draw the type of comics that went out of style 30 years ago. I would think it was funny if I wasn't afraid the same thing would happen to me.

I got hired to do a book with a wealthy woman about her time when she was locked up in an insane asylum. She is still insane as hell. She was uniquely irritating. The kind of person that was so lacking in self-awareness that everyone around her either lied to her and took advantage of her idiocy or told her the truth and fought with her. I chose the former.

I spent the summer sitting at her kitchen table while both of us pretended to work on the book as long as we could. We kept getting waylaid, though. A lot of what we did was try to figure out where a sound was coming from that only she could hear. She was pretty sure her parents were creating the noise in an effort to drive her mad. If they were, they sure as fuck succeeded. After a few months we both had to internally admit that we were frauds, although we had enough pride not to mention it to each other. I just stopped going there one day and haven't heard from her since.

I got a deal with another porn star. I went through Wikipedia and found a couple hundred of them. I sent like 50 of them emails pretending that I thought that their book would sell well. In reality I had no idea who any of them were. Eventually one bit and sent me a check to work with her. The check that I have 600 bucks left of. All I have done for a month is sit in a chair and write about cocks, pussies and assholes.

How many ways can one write about an asshole?

CHAPTER TWO

Of course many consider this wreck of a life that I lead romantic. I don't have alarm clocks going off, I work with these hot chicks that are famous for sucking cock, I spend a good portion of my time at a bar. Not just a bar. This bar. I don't find it romantic, but at times it is convenient. And it is much better to be poor than to have money and do something you don't want to do all day. You don't believe me. But it is.

I just finished my third vodka tonic and Brad is buying me a fourth. He is drinking beer. This disgusts me. This place pours like three shots of booze into every drink, and he is drinking beer? We go out for a smoke. Brad keeps talking about how much he is worried that his wife is going to smell the cigs on him. I have a little weed so he and I go around the corner to get high.

Brad likes to get high. I have Pineapple Express. At least that is what the guy I bought it off said I had. I don't care about shit like that. Brad talks and laughs. I space out. We come back in. There is some idiot at the bar in my seat. I ask him to move. He does, but just even the fact that I had to do so makes me tired. I want to go home. But not to the home I have. I want to go to another home from days gone by. Since this is not possible I start to pound down my fourth drink. Brad starts up again.

"So dude when you get done with this book what do you do then?"

"I write another book. I am working on a novel, but I keep getting stuck man. I can't come up with any good ideas that aren't about myself. Novels are hard, they take discipline, which I don't have. I just need to find another ghostwriting gig."

"Well, I ask for a reason."

Brad stopped and took another drink from his beer, then went on. "You remember that guy I was telling you about? The Westerburgers guy?"

Brad was always talking about this idiot he represents whose dad started Westerburgers, which was a huge hamburger chain around here. It was named after Paul Westerberg, the guy in the Replacements. The burgers all had names that were take offs on Replacements songs like "Pleased to Meat Me" and "You Be Me For Awhile and I'll Be Food."

The guy's name was Dylan Porter. He had been to numerous rehabs over time and Brad's job was basically to protect his financial interests and not have him get shut off. According to Brad, he got millions every year and did nothing but get hammered. He had been to drug rehab, alcohol rehab and even sex rehab. Who the fuck goes to sex rehab?

I nodded to Brad to acknowledge that I heard him. I know I probably should have actually said something but it took a lot effort to even do that.

Brad plowed on. "Well I was rapping with him the other day. He wants someone to write a book with him. I mean he said he did anyway, and when he says he wants to do something he usually does it."

This got my attention. I had been whoring around looking for more work for months. The porn well seemed to have dried up for now, and besides I was so sick of writing about cock sucking and assholes at this point that it was difficult to even explain. Sometimes I try to explain it to people, but honestly they don't seem that interested.

I also had heard through Brad that this guy was kind of a lunatic. This was my dream gig. I always had wanted to get a ghostwriting job with someone wealthy and insane. Not like "eating their own feces, stab me in the back when I am not looking" insane. I was thinking like someone rich that would shower me with money while we sat around and talked. Then I would write the crazy things they said down. Then I would try and sell the crazy book by the crazy rich person.

It was something that I thought about a lot. I thought I had that deal with the crazy rich woman I sat around the kitchen table with, but sadly she was a boring, crazy rich woman with no stories to tell. This dude sounded better than that.

I immediately got myself out of the whole "Jesus Christ Brad shut the fuck up" mindset and tried to put a serious expression on my face. "Really? Hook us up, man. I need work."

"Well, there are a couple things though. First off he isn't around anymore. He's in Samoa. Not the cute American Samoa either, he is in the other part, whatever the fuck that is called."

"Umm, it's called Western Samoa. That's cool man I can do all of this remotely, I don't need to actually sit down in a room with the dude."

Brad laughed a little. This bothered me. "Well that is it, he wants someone to sit down in a room with him. He wants someone to sit in a room with him for a month. And the other thing is, this isn't going to be like a memoir of his life, of how he got rich or anything like that. It is going to be about his spiritual journey, where he came from, where he is today. He wants to tell stories about his life before and then how he changed spiritually and what it is like now. The thing is the guy is fucking nuts. I wasn't even going to bring it up."

At this point I was feeling a tingling in my loins. I actually had to look down to make sure that the dude sitting to my left wasn't caressing my balls. Since he was not I continued on.

"Brad. Seriously. This stuff is what I do. Why don't you give me his email or something and we can move forward and I can see if it might be a good fit."

Brad took another swig off his beer. "I will do that, but listen here is the thing. The dude has been over in Samoa for quite a while now. It keeps him off the radar with his family."

"I think I told you but his dad remarried and his stepmom is always trying to get him cut off. She hates him. Being over there keeps him out of rehab too. His dad doesn't know what he is doing so he just does what he wants. He hangs over there, he chills out and he travels around the world and does these vision quests. What he wants is someone to write the story of his spiritual vision, of what he seeks, and what he finds when he does these things."

I was loving this. "Brad man, I would love to do that kind of thing. The thing is with me I might not be the greatest writer in the world but I get things done. You know how many people say they are going to write a book but they never do? I write books. If he hires me his book will get finished and I will find a publisher for it."

I always said shit like this. It was my elevator pitch.

Brad started to laugh.

This pissed me off. "What the fuck is so funny? I'm being serious."

Brad stopped. "Sorry man. Listen, it isn't what you said. It was the thought of this stuff getting published. The guy is a hard core sex addict. I mean I hate that term, sex addict, it sounds so stupid, but that is what he is. See the thing is, the reason he wants to write the book is what he says happened the last time he went on a quest."

"Right…go on." This was making me impatient. I wanted to go back to my place and email this guy tonight.

"Well I guess he went on this vision quest thing and he met God. Or not just God, but a bunch of beings that he called Gods."

"Brad…what is the point? I can work with anyone. No one freaks me out."

Brad started laughing again. "Well. I guess when he met the Gods? He said he fucked them."

CHAPTER THREE

December 11

8:40 AM

Dear Mr. Porter,

I hope you do not mind me writing you this way but I received your email from Brad Greyham. I have known Brad for quite a while now and he suggested that I get in touch with you.

Brad relayed to me that you may be looking for someone to work with on a book project.

I am a published writer of fiction as well as a ghostwriter. I have three books that I ghostwrote either published or under contract. My book with the famous adult film star Summer Starr will be out in June of this year.

I would be more than happy to send you some targeted writing samples if you wish. I write well, and I am professional. With that said, as I am new to the game, my cost is not as much as some of the more established ghostwriters.

I hope to hear from you with any questions that you might have.

Yours,

Brian Whitney

. . .

December 13

3:30 AM

Brian,

Listen I am not sure what Brad told you but that guy is a total fuckstick. I don't even pay for him you know. He acts like he is on my side but he is paid for by my father. There is no way in Hell that I would take his recommendation on anything. In fact when I got your email I laughed at you. I laughed at you that you thought that you could be someone that I would work with in any way. AHAHAHHAHAAHA. That is pretty much what I did.

I don't give a fuck about how cheap you are. I am totally rich. My place is fucking awesome and I do what I want all the time when I want to do it. I have two chicks that live here and lick my balls when I beat off. But they aren't whores or prostitutes. They just do it. And then usually I eat something and take a swim.

Now you might think that all sounds great, and it totally is, but the thing is I feel kind of empty. Sometimes it seems like there needs to be more than being in a big house and using a chick as a footstool while I read "Up in the Old Hotel," so I started studying about religions and spirituality and things got really wild.

So wild in fact that I need to write about it.

Now you might ask yourself why the Hell am I still writing you when I already said I think you are an idiot for writing me? For two reasons.

For one I read your fiction. You are really fucked up. And I don't mean that like it bothered me. I need someone that will just go where this takes us and will not question my scene. It is what it is and I want someone that just hangs with me and lets it flow. I think you could do that.

Secondly I really always wanted to fuck Summer Starr. I think it is so cool that you have banged her. I mean I also think it is kind of gross, I mean how many people have climbed that mountain you know? And what is she now like 50 years old or something? But seriously, whatever man you fucked Summer Starr. Even if it was at a time when nobody else wanted to. No one can take that away from you.

So here is the deal, you can come out here and hang out with me for a couple of weeks and we can do this shit. I like the fact that Brad is on board with you because that will make my family feel safe with it. Also I would like a photo of Summer Starr passed out, naked and wearing a moose hat.

Let me know if this works.

Dylan

...

December 13

6:03 AM

Dear Dylan,

I have to say I am really excited about this. The one thing is though we never talked terms or anything of the sort. Would you like me to send out a sample contract? What I usually do is work for a small amount up front and then I get a percentage of profits. Of course if you wish we could also just do a fee and you keep all of the royalties yourself. I like to get twenty percent, but I could get ten, it all depends.

Also I am not sure what you want to do, often the best way to do things is to just talk over the phone or on Skype and get a basic outline going? We could outline some chapters and then just kind of write back and forth and see if we could get things flowing.

Also I never had sex with Summer. She actually is a very nice lady and is still quite attractive. Ha.

Let me know how you want to proceed.

Brian

. . .

December 14

1:33 AM

Look Brian seriously I don't think you paid any attention to anything I said. First of all I just wired you 5 grand to your PayPal. We can talk about the rest of it when you get out here. I got you a ticket to fly into Samoa leaving a week from today.

You fly into LA first. I got you there for a night then you go out the next day. I seriously do want that passed out moose hat photo of Summer though. If you don't get it don't come out. That isn't some sort of test, I am not an asshole. Honestly I just don't think I like you as much as I thought I would if you don't get it. I have two girls I live with here, one of them is passed out right now wearing a fez. It is what it is. I fucking hate that expression but it seems to fit right now. You know what else I hate when people say? "It's all good." It never, ever, is all good.

Do not tell Brad shit. Tell him nothing. I did some research and I found out you live with a hot chick. Tell her as much as you want about me, but also tell her that when you get out here you will not be talking to her anymore. I don't mean ever for fucks sake, I mean for a month. What we are going to do is we are going to hang out for a week or two and you can sort of get my vibe and then we are going to go out and do the same kind of scene I did before and see what happens.

You are to write this as me. You are to be with me for every single fucking second from the time you get here until the time that you leave. I am not going to do a contract with you. I am not going to figure out what you are going to get paid. You are going to take my 5 grand and my plane ticket. You are going to get a picture of Summer passed out naked in a moose hat. You are going to stay with me for two months and be with me every second. I will tell you stories while you hang out here, you will write them down. Then we go out and find the Gods again and we see what happens.

We will figure out the rest later.

See you in a week. Someone will be at the airport to pick you up. Probably Staci. She has this really annoying laugh when she is nervous, she is white and she is tall. That should be enough for you to find her.

. . .

December 15

7:10 AM

Dylan,

Cool. I am down. I just checked my PayPal. Thank you. Listen though I have no idea how to get a picture of Summer passed out, naked in a moose hat. Honestly I probably could have sex with her, which takes care of the naked part but the passed out part with the hat I don't think I can do.

See you in a week.

Brian.

. . .

December 15

7:12 AM

Joey,

I am going to send you some roofies fed ex today. So that is that. We don't do excuses here Jerry.

Latte.

CHAPTER FOUR

My girlfriend wasn't psyched that I was leaving, but I know she was happy I finally made some money. I had been broke for a while now.

I had this part time job at one point working for AAA where I answered roadside assistance calls. I got fired for hanging up on people. I would do it in the middle of when I was talking so it looked like an accident. I did it whenever I couldn't figure something out on the computer system they had. I hate looking like an idiot.

Anyway I had been broke for a really long time. So she was cool with me going to Samoa even though she thought it rather odd.

We had been together for a few years now. I liked her fine, but I didn't really love her. Whatever that means. She was super hot but pretty much every time she started talking I would space right out. She had a nice laugh though, and most of the time she wasn't mean to me.

We both established I had a drinking problem because quite often when I was drunk I would tell her the truth about what I really thought about her and how I knew that she and I wouldn't work out. This, of course, meant that I was a nasty drunk, and not an honest one.

I didn't tell her that I wouldn't be talking to her for a month once I got to Samoa. That might seem odd but that is how I always operated with her. I never told her anything until I had to.

I said it would be a week, that this dude Dylan was just loaded, and wanted me to come out to work on a book, that I would be back soon, that I loved her and so on. I didn't tell her I was going to be gone for a month. I didn't tell her that hopefully I wasn't coming back. I mean, I would come back if I had to. I didn't like hurting people's feelings.

The morning before I left I got this email:

...

December 21

9:31 AM

Gorehound,

When the fuck are you going to be here? Well, I know when you are coming I bought you your ticket, but I mean the metaphorical when, and I don't really mean anything by the word "here."

But man time is wasting. I am dying here, by degrees. We all get older. It happens to all of us. It does. The cool guy of today is the married guy in the suburbs of tomorrow.

I am going to tell you a story to illustrate this. It can be in my book. It will be in my book. Change the names though, I am not stupid. This is the kind of thing I want you to do. Take this and make it better.

Brad said you knew my buddy Tim. I loved Tim. He showed up in Portland at some point under shady circumstances but I accepted him anyway. I am prone to do things like that. Rumor was that he killed some chick in a sleeping bag by hitting her with a girl in a sleeping bag. Regardless, when I met him he was a peach.

I remember the first time I saw him he was eating the intestines of a live waitress at Bull Feeneys. He dipped them in the orange sauce between bites, you know the kind that they do with the chicken fingers. He then performed a pretty amazing surgery right there on the table, he took about half of his own intestines (don't forget we each have like 3 miles in us or something like that) and replaced hers with his. It was kind of a gross M.C. Escheresque deal, because her intestines were in his being digested and... well, you can imagine how trippy it was at the time. Anyway, he stitched her up and asked her out right then. She of course said yes, they fucked right on the spot, and ended up getting married 14 months later.

Tim being a married man, what a total shock that was to all of us! Gone were the nights of us banging random people in bowling alleys, hunting snails with limes and showing up for auditions at Lucid Stage stoned on opium with our clothes soaked in owl's blood. Instead we found ourselves having potlucks with new friends that we met at Plush, and knitting sweaters for local rape victims. We're getting old. Next thing you know Tim doesn't call me back for weeks, I get married to a set of hot twins who won't let me try on the pink sock with either of them ever, and gray hairs start arriving in my beard like unwelcome whores in your mother's church. I basically spend all my time sitting around, smoking the brown frown and giving myself a low five.

Then August 12th came along.

I woke up, drunk as usual and called in sick to work. I was doing something important back then, I was president of something or other, or captain of a fleet of ships maybe. I can't remember. Anyway, I called in sick and was laying there wondering who was going to be on Dr. Phil, when I just had a thought. What is that rascal Tim doing right this second?

I decided not to call and warn him that I was showing up, I just piled into my ride and drove to Lewiston where Tim was working as a salesman for Lewiston Auburn magazine. That magazine doesn't exist anymore because the publisher got caught looking at kiddie porn. I don't think that would have mattered so much except he was a prick. No one, but no one likes a guy that is a total dick and also likes to bang kids. Remember that.

Anyway, I roared up the turnpike to his building and walked around until I saw Tim. There he was, hunched over, pale and pasty from the fluorescent tubes that were his only solar nourishment, and obviously attempting to hide a huge erection in his pants. I quietly walked up behind him and tapped him on the shoulder and did my best boss imitation. "Tim, what is that you have on your screen there?" and he turned around and killed me.

Killed me dead, right there. He smashed my face in with the keyboard; I was dead within 10 seconds. He realized pretty quick who I was and what he had inadvertently done, and he immediately yelled "Osama Bin Laden!" and everyone came and gutted me and hung me up on a pole and it was broadcast around the world. He got a 2 million dollar reward for killing me, and took that and travelled the world for 4 years with the sole mission of laying a woman of every nationality and ethnicity before setting foot back into Portland.

At some point he brought me back to life. I can't remember exactly how, he did something with hair gel and a pumpkin. We don't hang out much anymore.

So seriously get the picture of that old jizzbag with the hat on. See you Wednesday Dilly.

Dylan

CHAPTER FIVE

It wasn't as hard as it sounded. I thought it would be, but it wasn't. In actuality the whole thing was easy.

I hit Los Angeles on the way to Samoa. I didn't get a hotel room. I was going to stay with Summer, she just didn't know it yet. People usually let you stay with them if you're drunk and in trouble, and that was what was going to happen tonight.

I used to have a car that had a headlight out. I would go out and drink with different women and once I got kind of buzzed and we were having a good time I would make the move. "Hey I really don't want to split but I have a headlight out, I have to leave before it gets dark or I am gonna get pulled over."

Then the woman would say, "oh well you can stay with me if you need to, I have a couch." Then three hours later I would be banging her from behind and doing a puppet show with her ass.

I meet Summer for a drink when I get to L.A., her book is out soon and it gives me an excuse. She still is kind of hot for an old chick, but the fact that she is an old chick that has fucked thousands of guys is not a big turn on for me.

I don't get that anyway. I mean why is that hot? Why would I want to fuck some chick that has had two thousand dicks in her? And besides, I wrote her book, I spent months hunched over a chair in a tiny apartment writing about her sexual exploits and how much she loved to fuck.

So we drink, and we drink more and it doesn't take me long to get in with her for the night. In fact all I did is mention there was a screw up with my reservation and she said I could stay at her house. In my pocket I have some roofies, and in my bag I have a moose hat. You might be asking yourself, "Where the hell did you get a moose hat?" I live in Maine. Moose hats are easy.

So we drink a lot and we eat a little and we talk about promotions and what happens next. I know what happens next, but I don't think she does. What happens is she goes on Howard Stern, and talks about how many people she has banged. I spend my days researching sex blogs on the net and writing them asking if they will review her book. She will make 20 grand, I will make 5. That's what happens.

We cab it back to her place and she is drunk. I need to time this right, of course. If I do it too late Summer will be sucking on my cock and possibly expecting me to bang her. This is not me being conceited. She is who she is.

If I do it too early, then she wakes up the next day and asks herself: "Umm, why did I pass out at 9 and sleep for 24 hours?"

We sit outside on her deck and we talk while we drink. I bring out the bottle of vodka, and I keep filling our cups, although I am not drinking anymore, just she is. When she leaves to go to the bathroom I switch our cups so hers is always full. After an hour or two she is hammered. When she goes off to get some smokes, I drop the roofies into her drink.

She comes back soon and lights up and slurs out the words, "and what was I saying darling?"

"You were talking about custom videos. How you have been doing more of them lately."

She smiled and went on. "Right. Lately I do custom videos. I thought I would try them. Why not?"

"I don't know much about them," I say.

"Well, a custom video is when a man, or sometimes a woman, writes me and asks me to film a video just for them. This means that the things they like to see are not regularly available to the general public. That is a nice way of putting it. Another way to put it is that these people are freaks. I don't judge people, mind you. I never do. People write me emails, and they ask me to do things. I get paid money of course. I don't do things just because they ask. That would be ridiculous."

She laughed. "They pay me to do the things that the women in their world would never do. Quite often the person has written a script for me to follow. Other times they just have an idea. They pay me and I do what they want me to do."

I started to watch her carefully as she slurped her drink. It seemed like she was starting to slur a bit more as she went on.

"If it is bondage you like, if it turns you on to see me helpless and tied up, bound and gagged, you can find that quite easily on the net. But if you want to see me chloroformed and carried, or if you want to see me passed out while someone plays with my feet or jiggles my boobs, you might have to do a custom. I used to do all sorts of necro stuff. Don't knock it until you've tried it. It's easy money playing dead for the camera. And I can't even count how many times I have been a super heroine who has been hypnotized and turned into a slave. I can say 'Yes, Master' in my sleep. I get kidnapped a lot, and of course I get raped."

I was wondering when she was going to pass out. I had never drugged anyone before. "So I guess what you are saying is these dudes, these guys that write you, have rather odd or extreme tastes."

She shrugged. "Some of them just want me to humiliate them. I do a lot of POV work. This is where I just talk into the camera about what a disgusting little worm you are. How you're a money pig. How you're pathetic. How tiny your little cock is. How I am going to shop on your dime while you kneel in front of me and jerk off with your credit card in your mouth."

"One man just wants me to crush bugs with my feet. He wants me to put on nylons and crush some bugs. That's all. Another wants me to itch. A burglar breaks in while I shower and puts itching powder all over my clothes. Then I get dressed and go to a business meeting. And I itch. Oh, I itch so fucking much. That's pretty much it."

She went on. "Or I can be a stripper tiger. One guy wanted that. Being a sexy tiger is way harder than it sounds. I put on a tiger stripe leotard and I hump the floor. A man pats my head and rubs my ass. He puts water in a bowl for me to drink out of."

"Shall I be a robot? Maybe you have a remote control and I can walk around, all robot-like until you press a button. Then I stop. Until you press the button again. Until then I am just a helpless robot."

I laughed. Now I wasn't sure I even wanted her to pass out. I could probably just ask her to put on the moose hat. "Right, everyone wants to fuck a robot."

"Darling, I know! How about this? A man wants me to be naked on my back. He wants a fat man to sit on me. The fat man says, 'I am going to squish you.' He says that for fifteen minutes or so. That's the whole video. In another one, I'm naked and I have a bowling ball stuck on my big toe. Or I put on panty hose that control my mind. They not only control my mind, they turn me into an infant. I lie on the floor kicking my legs in the air and making baby sounds. I say 'Someone help me! These pantyhose keep forcing me to be a baby. Before long I will be trapped as a baby forever!'

"I get murdered. I get choked. I date men who turn out to be serial killers. They kill me and play with my feet. A man writes and wants to pay me to have my face peed on. He ends his missive with, 'Thanks for your time.'

"It gets a little confusing sometimes. My fans tell me they love me, and yet they write me and want the most horrible things to happen to me."

The last two minutes, Summer has been slurring like crazy. I stand up.

"That is so crazy. It's like if someone had this fantasy to see you passed out and naked wearing a moose hat."

Her eyes were starting to close. "That would be mild compared to the things I've done."

I nodded. "It seems that way. Listen, I have to take a leak."

She waved her hand. She settled deep into her chair.

I waited about five minutes before I came back. She was out. Her jaw was slack and she was already snoring.

CHAPTER SIX

The photos themselves were a bit of a letdown. I was wasted and it was a total pain in the ass to take off all her clothes. It was harder than I thought it would be. I mean of course I was turned on a little, I gave her ass a few proprietary slaps here and there, but for the most part it was just clothes off, moose hat on, pose her body this way and that, take some photos, clothes back on.

I had about ten texts from my girlfriend about how much she missed me. This made me feel bad. I did like her but when I was away or when she was away I didn't even really notice it.

Summer was still out cold next to me. At one point I dragged her into her bedroom and slept next to her in bed. I imagined she would probably be out for another five hours or so at least. I wrote her a note about how much I appreciated her letting me stay and left it next to her on the pillow.

I put the moose hat under her bed and fired up her laptop. Her email was open. There were a lot of sad ones to some guy. They were about how much she missed him and how she wished things were different.

I logged out of her account and into mine. There was an email from him.

. . .

December 23

2:45 AM

Napster,

I just kicked out my roomie because I am expecting you tomorrow. So you better show up because it was a huge fucking pain in the ass getting him out of here. I have had like 30 roomies here, or maybe 3.

My first roomie was a guy named Joe. Joe laughed a lot, pretty much all the time really. That is what I remember about him the most, was him just looking at me and laughing. I know that sounds really fun and for the most part it was.

I met Joe when he showed up at my place. He came with his bags and said that it was nice to meet me and that he was my new roomie and that he was sure we would get on fine. Then he laughed.

And things would have been fine except that he used to steal from me. He would take money out of my wallet and one time he took my toothbrush and hid it in his shoe. He would do these things when I was looking right at him. I cannot even tell you how fucking angry that kind of shit made me.

One time he told me that he was going to drink and take a lot of pills and that he might not wake up for a couple of days but whatever I did I shouldn't call an ambulance. I said okay.

The next morning he didn't wake up, or the morning after that. A lot of me was worried sick all day but in another way it was almost less worrisome just having him there without stealing from me. That shit seriously made me mad. On the third day he woke up. As soon as he did he got up and unplugged the clock radio, put it in his duffel bag and walked out the door.

Finally I told him that he had to leave. When I did, he grabbed me and put me in a headlock and gave me an Indian sunburn and pulled me down on the bed with him and then we wrestled for a really long time. We wrestled pretty much the entire night. Most of the time I was pretty angry about it, but then he would giggle and it wouldn't be that bad. He left first thing in the morning but he took my keys and also a painting of a cat that I had been working on for a really long time. The cat was laying on its side in the sun and had its eyes sort of half open. I was almost done with it.

Joe would still come over every once in a while. He still had a set of keys although sometimes he would just come over and bang on the door and not let himself in. Other times he would use his key and come in and make me dinner. He would say things like "Who wants pot roast?" And then when I would say that sounded nice he would just go through my wallet and leave. One night I killed him because of this. I won't bore you with the details, this is about people that lived in my house, not people that are dead.

Finally Glenn moved in. We would sit around and we would talk about things. He would say things like "you don't have to be a writer to know how that story ends." You know, stuff that would really make you think. He would tell jokes. I would tell him that he should be a comedian and he would smile and tell some more. There were some jokes that he told about a squirrel that used to work as a stock boy at a department store that really would make me laugh.

At one point he moved into the bathroom so we each could have our own space and when Joe came over one night and tried to steal my toothbrush, Glenn jumped out from his shower bed and yelled "Gotya!!!!" Really loud. Joe shat himself right on the spot and then laughed and laughed until me and Glenn laughed too.

Of course this was before I killed Joe, and now I had to kick Glenn the fuck out because of you.

PS. Robin Williams killed himself because he didn't want to do Mrs. Doubtfire 2. What the fuck. MRSDF2 4LYFE.

See you tomorrow.

Dylan

. . .

It was time to go. I took 40 bucks out of Summer's wallet for cab fare, kissed her on the forehead, and headed for the airport.

CHAPTER SEVEN

I drank a lot on the flight. I was kind of nervous. Well, nervous isn't the right word. That would make it sound like I actually cared about things. But I was unsettled.

I sat in the middle between a really hot chick and a guy that was kind of sweaty and looked like he was on acid. The chick took some pills and passed out during takeoff. She was out for ten hours. Her mouth was wide open the whole time. I wanted to play with her tongue, but I thought that might be considered untoward.

I was just about to fire up my laptop when the sweaty guy started talking to me. "Man I sure am tired."

I turned to look at him a bit. "Umm, yeah. Me too."

He went on. "I barely got any sleep at all last night. I guess I was nervous about the flight and then I couldn't sleep, so I started having some people by and then more people kept stopping over and before long it was like 5 in the morning. I started nodding off this morning while driving the bus and I hit the rumble strip a bit and the kids started screaming and yelling like they were on fire or something. It was funny as shit."

"Ha," I said. "What are you doing in Samoa?"

"I am going there to help the Pride Parade. My life was a mess before Charlie Pride, man. I just shit on anything and everything, I didn't want to go to college, I had shit to do. I traveled all through the country lying cheating and stealing, it was like the world was my bowling alley and I was like a big fucking bowling ball. Except you know when I knocked all the pins down I didn't just fall down a hole and disappear. I was still there with the pins lying down all around me. Although in reality I wasn't really still there. Anyway I think you get the picture, right?"

I stared at him.

"I'll tell you what I mean," he said. "I had a very close and dear friend who I used to camp, hike, go to concerts, and trip with. Little did I know that what I had believed to be a recreational and harmless good time was much more than that for him. I seldom did more than smoke pot and take LSD, do some coke, a benzo here and there and sometimes shrooms. My friend on the other hand, had somehow gotten into using vinegar to break down crack and then would shoot it into his arm. I knew nothing about this until it was too late."

"One summer he and I had rented a cabin in Northern Wisconsin. We had taken a few ounces of shrooms with us as we had the place for a week. The first night we were there we had both eaten a fair amount of mushrooms each. I remember that I kept seeing spirits coming out of the lights and worms crawling in and out of the walls."

"My friend went into the bathroom at some point. I have no idea how long he had been there because I was distracted by so many things. I do remember that after a while I became concerned and went to check on him. That's when I found out about his secret habit. There was a spoon on the sink and a needle on the floor, a film canister full of vinegar on the tank behind the toilet and a wad of cotton next to it. My friend was motionless in the corner with some kind of liquid coming out of his mouth. He had had a heart attack, he was dead."

"I don't remember what happened next, but I do know that I was too spun out to use a phone let alone deal with the stringent amount of authority that was sure to follow this situation. So I didn't. I just stayed with him. For the whole week. I loved him so much I just didn't know what else to do. I believe it's what he would've wanted. I was really out of my mind."

"I ate the rest of the shrooms by myself and had one final rage with my friend. When it was all over I found all these pictures I had taken of him in all these different poses. I even put a different shirt on him every day… I didn't want to take his pants off. I had pictures of him propped up under a tree beneath a setting sun, pictures of him with his hand in a bowl of trail mix and a deck of cards on the table in front of him, I even blew smoke into his mouth so that I could see him hit the blunt just one last time."

"I know that it sounds crazy… if you've never been in the situation. But when you really love somebody, it's just so fucking hard to let go. I haven't been the same since he left. Have you ever done that?"

I was boggled. "What? Hung out with a dead friend?"

He plowed on. "So after this I went off the deep end for a bit. I wound up with the clap and spent all my money in this fetish whorehouse down in Mexico. I ended up hitching to El Paso, which is where I saw Charlie Pride for the first time. He was singing 'when the snakes crawl at night' and I got to talk to him after the show. Since then I have been a changed man. I got a job driving a bus for the school district now and all the kids love me. I ain't like their parents. I am more like a buddy. I have been in the Pride Parade like three or four months now."

At this point I didn't think things were going to get weirder and I thought he was winding down a bit. "That is awesome," I said.

He continued. "When I was born I was brought into life as the son of little folk just like you. I was simple. I knew not what I missed. We worshiped Jesus and yet every day we saw nothing but rain. Each morning I touched the rain and each night I thought that the rain would stop, but it kept on. Not only this but even as a child I knew my parent's God told me things that were not true."

"Later on, as an adult, I became a bumbler. I had become angry at the ways of the little folk. They had shown me rain and I wanted sunshine or I wanted thunder. But rain was all I saw. I put heroin in my arm, I played guitar, and I listened to a band called Cows. I saw thunder every day, and every night the lightning would crash into my room and frighten me. I cheated on every woman that trusted me and all of them did."

"I continued to bumble. My wife threw me out of my home because she found out that I had moved in with another woman. This punishment seemed truly unfair and the spike moved from my arm to my groin. I soon was reduced to dealing meth outside of the county fairgrounds. Every night I would try and turn little folk into bumblers and every night I would succeed."

"One night I heard a sound and I stopped in my tracks. It was Charlie Pride (I call him Charley). His voice was strong and kind and as he sang the words 'I got a ticket to Misoury,' my mind cleared and I knew that I must meet this man, this prophet. This leader."

"Since the moment of our meeting I have walked beside him but never in front. You little folk may walk beside me until you are in his presence and then you will crawl, once you crawl you float, until you can walk again Charlie will teach you the way. Your children will die, but you will understand it. His soft hands will touch your face and you will learn."

"We have 200,000 members in Europe. We have 150,000 members in South America. Soon we will have America."

CHAPTER EIGHT

At this point I fired up my laptop and put my ear buds in. I wasn't even polite about it. Fuck this. Seriously.

Sadly if I was looking for sanity I didn't find it. The plane had in-flight wifi. And I had a new email from Dylan.

. . .

December 24

5:45 AM

Dilly.

I have been keeping a diary of daily events. Well, I only write in it about once every few weeks, and it isn't representative at all of who I am, or any fucking thing that is going on in my life. In fact I wrote it like 15 years ago. But regardless please read this. This will be something I will be looking for your help in rewriting.

Staci will be there to pick you up. Remember she is tall and has a nervous laugh. She likes to be told how unattractive she is. I am not joking. Tell her she is ugly and that you wish I had sent someone better and she will be yours while I am here. In fact she is going to be yours while I am here anyway. I am keeping Rita for myself. You can have Staci. I barely fuck Staci and haven't for quite a while now, so don't be grossed out.

As I said I wrote this in high school. I don't care though. It doesn't all have to be new material. I sort of want this to come out like Donnie Darko, except I want it to be a book and kind of emo. Like Donnie Darko meets the Graduate with a little Alex Chilton thrown in with some Kafka. Also I want it to be street. Kind of like KRS-1 meets Ice-Cube, but the nice Ice-Cube that was in Barbershop 2, not the one that hung out with Ren and talked about killing people. That stuff doesn't play as well as it used to.

Latte.

…

He had attached a Word document to the email. This is it in its entirety:

Jan 23

Everyone in this lame fucking town is always calling me up looking for drugs. My phone never stops ringing. It's bullshit all day long. The other day I was laying in bed having a play date with my best friend and just when I was about to release the hostages Todd calls. Todd is all "what's up and shit?" He says this to show me he's like down with my scene, even though he drives his Mom's Saab all around town, listens to fucking Dead bootlegs all the time, and has been accepted to Dartmouth. He has like long 70's hair and listens to the Doors. Around here he passes for counterculture. He's not street, not even a little.

So anyway he says he wants a dime and he's talking all quiet on the phone so his Mom doesn't hear him. First of all, who says a dime anymore? I felt like I was on fucking Magnum PI or something, secondly that's not nearly enough for me to make any coin off, but the thing is Todd's mom is hot. Her name is Mrs. Johnson. Every time I go over there she's like hammered off wine and pills, and is obviously completely miserable. Like she wants to die.

Its fucking sexy as Hell, all she does all day is drive her Jag to the store, drink wine and pop Xanax. I know she has Xanax cuz I go through her purse when I'm over there. One time I walked out of her place with a pair of her sandals sticking out of my back pocket and she didn't even notice. Another time I was over there and she was totally wasted. She had like crusties in her eyes and something dried up in the corner of her mouth. I was so turned on I couldn't even take it.

Anyway, I'm so not going to ride my bike all the way downtown just to make like ten bucks. This is the scene. I don't deal. I'm saying this to everyone not just Todd. Unless I can make a bill, I'm out.

. . .

April 17

I am so sick of the scene around here. It's nothing but fucking L.L. Bean boot-wearing assholes named Brad and brewpubs with beers named after the seasons. It's the kind of town where chicks with tight asses jog with baby carriages. Even the whores aren't ugly. Everyone's all into fucking emo, Abercrombie and knitting clubs.

I want it to be like it used to be. I want to live where a woman's ass jiggles for at least a minute after you slap it. I want to be able to urinate in public. You can't even get cheap weed. Everyone around here listens to Phish and smokes out of chillums. Since my dad busted me I can't afford a fucking 300 dollar Z and I'm riding my three speed around smoking the brown frown in my bowl, which isn't even made of fucking glass while Ian and Zack drive by in their goddamn Saab smokin' the kindies.

Fuck this. People don't understand me around here. I don't want a job. I just want weed, booze, ass and cable. I want mad respect when I'm steppin' out. But most of these chicks around here are haters.

. . .

May 3

I love how your eyes bulge when you wake up
with me sucking on your toes, while your husband sleeps beside you.

When we go out you always pretend you don't know me
when I give you the signal.

I adore how absentminded you are with your arthritis pills,
the neighborhood kids pay five bucks a pop for them.

When you wrap your stringy thighs around my ears
I feel like I am being taken by death to another realm.

I love how you pretend you don't know I'm stealing from you.
Thanks.

Your feet smell like heaven,
and when I slap your ass I feel like it will jiggle forever.

I appreciate the rides to the mall more than you know,
and thanks for never asking questions when I need to hide in
your basement for a few days.

Baby, I love you

...

June 1

I didn't go home last night. Yesterday I was just chilling out
listening to the sound of one hand clapping when Mrs. Johnson
called. She's all "Hey can you come over?" and I'm like "Isn't it a

little late and shit? Isn't your husband coming home soon?" But she's all "No he's going to be at a meeting until like 7 or something and I miss you." So I'm like "I'll come over but I'm kind of faded, and I'm not down for too much." So I hung up, finished badgering the witness and rolled on over there. My bike has a fucking flat though so I had to walk. It sucked.

So I get there and right away I can tell something is off. Last time she gave me like a hoodie and a 25 dollar gift certificate to Applebee's though, so I'm gonna ride this shit out. As soon as I get in there she's all, "Yay Daddy is home, let me take your briefcase!" and "Did you have a hard day? I wish you could sit down and relax, but the baby has been very bad and I think you are going to have to spank him while I watch," and all this shit. So I'm thinking she just wants to watch me make the bald guy cry but no dude she takes me in the bedroom and who do I see but Mr. Fucking Johnson. Wearing a diaper.

So anyway I did it. I mean I fucking did it for hours. He was screaming and crying and Mrs. Johnson was like yelling, "Bad Baby, Bad Baby" and I'm spanking him and all like, "I work all fucking day and come home to this shit!"

When I left I just walked around and shit. I ended up going down to the wharf and just like sitting and thinking about my life and what it had become until the sun came up. Tonight's going to rock, though. I'm like so totally going to Applebee's.

. . .

June 3

It fucking sucks around here. There's nothing to do. All I've been doing all week is sitting around roughing up the suspect and watching Ridiculousness on MTV. Even if you go to a bar, it's all dead, like no scene at all. It's totally impossible to rub up against a chick's ass without her knowing about it, the other night I was out on the floor poppin' and lockin' on 80's night to "Wild Wild West" by Kool Moe Dee and I look around and I'm the only one on the fucking floor and shit. Fuck. I just went home and practiced for the big game.

The scene with chicks is way different too. I haven't gotten laid in like two weeks. Even Mrs. Johnson doesn't want to fuck anymore. I mean I like the free clothes and shit, but it's a total drag going over there three times a day and making sure she hasn't escaped her chains and feeding her cheese. It sucks. I have her blindfolded and gagged and I'm spanking her ass and screaming and I'm watching the "Price is Right" with the sound down over her shoulder. I know it sounds hot but I don't even get off on it anymore.

So I've been drinkin'. And I've been thinkin.' I mean what the fuck. How the fuck did this happen to me? I'm not sure if it's the pills but sometimes I close my eyes and it's all swirly and back to front ways. It's like I know who I am but I can't get past it. There isn't a purpose anymore, it's just like chasing that next high and that next fucking orgasm and every day I wake up and I'm like today I'm going to get my shit together but I can't, cuz I'm so fucking scared of it, and what the fuck is it anyway? I mean I can't fucking touch it, I just know it's there and it's fucking floating, and I can see it float but I can't fucking touch it.

. . .

June 17

I'm so fucking tired of Mrs. Johnson. I swore I wasn't going to go back over there, not for like anything. I don't need to roll like that. I'll just get a job. I rode my three speed out by the mall the other day and filled out an application to be a bartender at TGI Fridays. I even talked to the manager dude, he was wearing this hat with like all these pins on it like "I'm with stupid!" and "It's all Good."

I mean what the fuck does that mean? It's all good? Like even when I'm totally wasted and getting my sack lapped it's still not all good, not fucking all of it. I mean maybe the chick lapping my sack has like huge hair and I can't see the TV over her shoulder and I miss the end of Survivor. I was way too faded to like pay attention to anything he was saying, but I'm pretty sure I got the job.

Just in time too, I'm totally broke, my business took a mad hit. I was selling these kids in junior high school Oxycontin. Well really they were Flintstones Chewables I painted white. I'd like be playing "Animals" by Pink Floyd really fucking loud and I'd be swaying back and forth a little to make them feel like they were tripping their balls off. It was all good until Tad's brother told him that oxys weren't chewable.

But of course I went back. She called and I was starving. Mrs.

Johnson has those hot pockets that are like ham and cheese sammys except all hot and shit like that.

So I'm there like 5 minnies and she's like "I've been bad" and I'm all "me too" but then she's all "I need my daddy to teach me to be good, I need him to spank me, and draw a Fu Manchu mustache on my face with a magic marker while I sing 'I'm a little teapot.' I'm all "fuck." It is the same thing every time. Every time. I mean I admit the Fu Manchu and 'I'm a little teapot' are mad hot and shit but the whole time I was spanking her I was staring at that hot pocket. Hopefully that dude calls tomorrow.

...

July 3

Dude last winter fucking sucked. First of all we totally got douched with snow, like this is the type of town where as soon as it starts snowing everyone gets all cheerful and people are like skiing down the middle of the roads and smiling and pulling their kids around on sleds and shit like that. The whole scene totally pisses me off.

So I'm fucking stuck here all weekend, not just stuck here but stuck here jonesing my ass off. I mean first of all I'm out of smokes, secondly I've got no weed at all and I'm starting to think that maybe I shouldn't have stolen all of Mrs. Johnson's Percodans.

Well I mean stealing them was fine, she totally owes me for last time. I've still got a rash that won't go away. What I mean is maybe I shouldn't have been like eating ten a day for the last week, cuz I'm all out and it feels like weasels are chewing at my eyeballs and every time I look in the mirror my face looks like my mother's, well kind of like what I would imagine my mother would look like if some fucking spider had entered her body through her ear hole and had laid millions of little spider eggs and then all those eggs hatched and there were like tons of baby spiders crawling around in her brain and shit like that. What I'm saying is I'm kind of stressed.

And I can't fucking get off. I've been laying here for hours on end giving myself a low five and nothing. It's like I'm almost getting there and its beautiful. I'm like on my bed and watching Next while I'm clocking this one chick who is like totally naked except for this blue cowboy hat and these funky green shoes spinning a lariat all slack jawed, and this other chick is like my table at the foot of the bed and I keep reaching out and like eating cheetos off her and there's this orange soda in the middle of her back and the more I drink the fuller it gets and Mrs. Johnson is like off in the distance I can't see her but I can hear her "do you want me to cut the crust off your ham sammy?" and I know it's close and I can feel it, it's time to free the hostages, then like nothing.

I totally need a smoke.

. . .

August 13

Nothing ever happens in this fucking town. I feel so trapped. Like every day is like the last one. Get up, play a quick game of one man tug of war, watch Judge Judy, then smoke some nugs, have some Oreos or something, take a nap, choke Charlie until he throws up, watch Judge Joe Brown. Same fucking thing. Night time is different, all sorts of weird shit happens, it's always all swirly, and freaky styly and shit.

So what the fuck am I supposed to do when Mrs. Johnson calls today? She's all "Cal what's up? Can you come over?" I'm all "Yo Mrs. Johnson, you're harshin on my mellow, step off, I'm not hangin' with you no more, besides I got crabs or somethin." Not really yo, I'm just sick of her scene and all. But then she's like "but Cal, I bought you that hoodie you liked and I went to the mall the other day and saw these Pumas I could get for you."

So ten minutes later I'm knocking at her door. Unfortunately she wants to play door to door salesman. This is one of my least favorite games as it involves me touching her. Like a lot. First I have to talk my way in the door, then she makes me tea, then we sit down at the table, and I break the tea pot over her head. Then I have to tie her up with the drapes, stuff her underwear in her mouth and shake her tits around and yell. The cool thing is I blindfold her too, so I can read while I do it. It's a cool hoodie, though. Tomorrow I'm gonna change things up and sleep until noon or something.

...

That was the end of the document. What the hell? He wants to try and publish this shit? I hadn't seen anything this bad since I got hired to write a "How to Start a Restaurant" book by a guy who did not know how to spell the word "dining." By the time I finished reading there was another email.

. . .

December 24

8:00 AM

Dilly,

Fuck that diary. I don't want it in there. I was 12 when I wrote it. I was going for a word count. My bad. Staci just left to pick your ass up.

CHAPTER NINE

I flew into Faleolo Airport. I knew it was going to be small but I wasn't quite prepared for the lack of activity when I got there. The place was kind of what I expected other than that. Pinkish. Lovely. People were bustling around in an adorable way.

I got my bag and looked around. I saw her right away. She was tall, almost 6 feet with reddish long hair, pulled back into a ponytail. Not quite pretty, but not unattractive. She had a goofy smile on her face and was looking around nervously.

I walked up to her. "Staci?"

As soon as I said her name she laughed, in the most awkward way. We shook hands and walked to the car, which was a VW Golf. I expected something a bit more impressive, but being from Maine I am used to the island car.

When we got in the car she told me we were only going to be driving about forty minutes. We drove down a winding road, many houses we passed were put together with palm fronds, and the ones that were built in a more traditional way were still quite modest. Staci told me that the house where I would be staying had all the modern amenities, but it was obvious that it was not going to be the mansion that I may have anticipated.

"You're actually the first one to ever come visit, and we've been out here for a year or so." She laughed awkwardly again.

"Really?" I said. "What about all the roomies?"

She looked at me oddly. "We haven't had any roomies."

Okay. No roomies. So he lied about that. I plunged on, not really missing a beat. "Anyway, the whole thing is wild. How did you happen to get out here?"

"Well, I met Dylan a long time ago. He told me to tell you everything on the way to the house about how we met, for background for the book, so that is what I am going to do. He also wants you to know that anything you tell me to do I will do without question." She laughed again. It was the sort of laugh that one makes when lying about covering up a murder.

I looked at her. "Anything?"

"Yes." She replied.

"All right," I said. "Let's do it up."

"Okay. First I want to tell a story about when I dated Hemingway, it will give you a little background on me."

I was like, "You dated Hemingway. Oh."

Was everyone crazier than me now? I was not used to this. I was supposed to be the fucked up one.

She laughed in a goofy way. "Not the real Hemingway, of course. His name was Douglas. And I loved him. Of course I did. But Douglas was Hemingway of course, in just the way that only the very young, and very privileged could be."

"The world was a jail and we were going to break it together. That is what Hadley said to Hemingway. She did. She was his first wife, Hadley was. When he married her he was just 22. A babe!"

"So that was me. I was Hadley. Well at the time I was. I was no longer home. My father didn't have the ability to come into my room at night anymore. He didn't have me drive him around when he was too drunk, he didn't tell me how nice my body was, or ask to take naked photos that he could send his friends. He couldn't. I had left him and had left my mother, my silly, silly mother, and I was with Douglas."

"Your dad sounds like a total dick," I said.

" No. He was just rich. When you are rich people don't tell you that you're a dick. So it really isn't your fault if you act like one. Douglas was also 22, he was also rich, he was lovely, and he was mine. As much as he could be since in fact he was Hemingway."

I started to look out the window. "Yeah you told me. Hemingway."

"He wrote horrid poetry and passable short stories. I thought they were brilliant. We had sex. A lot. We drank and we did coke and we talked. We talked about so many things."

"He would say to me, quite often he would, that we must live as Hemingway did. I was never quite clear on what that meant, but it did mean something to him and that was all that really mattered to me at that point. I just wanted to be what someone else wanted me to be."

"I was his partner in crime. We spent so much time talking about the fools around us. How they were constrained in this life that we were not. They sought careers, and achievements and marriages. These things meant nothing to Hemingway."

"Those things don't mean anything to me either, but I don't go around calling myself Hemingway." I was spacing out. I didn't care about Hemingway. The flight was long, I sat next to a fucking lunatic the whole time, and now I was with this big goofy chick telling me a story about some pretentious dick.

She went on without responding. "There was this one woman. Douglas called her the Harpy. She wanted him. We both laughed at this. We did. But it also intrigued him that we could do what we wanted with her. That she was so malleable. So silly. He was in fact sure that he could get this foolish woman to have sex with us both."

"So one night we all got very drunk. Oh so drunk in fact. And we fucked. Douglas and I and this silly woman, this woman that meant nothing, and it was odd. Our bodies all together and me doing things that I would never have done if it wasn't for the fact that I was with Hemingway. At one point we were both laying on our bellies with our hands tied behind our backs at the edge of the bed while he took turns entering us both. The only thing that kept me going was I knew what was going on and the Harpy didn't."

"So it ended and I slept. I slept a deep drunken sleep. When I woke I was alone. But I heard some sounds down the hall, and I saw some light. And when I came upon them both fucking in a bedroom a few doors down, I cried. Hemingway never would have done that to me."

She stopped right then and drove on for a bit. I didn't really get it, so I said, "And that guy was Dylan?"

"No, I just liked the story. Wasn't that a good story?"

I laughed. "Yeah, it was pretty good actually. So, uh, listen… where do these vision quests happen? I didn't know Samoans did vision quests. Can you tell me about them?"

She looked at me. "Samoans don't do vision quests. Not as far as I know. Anyway, when I met Dylan I was still living with my boyfriend, a different one, not Hemingway. Dylan was living with his girlfriend as well. My boyfriend and I were buddies. We would talk together and have Indian food and watch TV. We didn't fuck much anymore. When I did it was sort of like having sex with my brother. The sort of thing that you just sort of closed your eyes and did so that for the next month or so you could think to yourself, 'We just fucked a week or so ago,' so then you didn't have to do it again. Because you just did."

I'd had one of those relationships, so I got it. "Been there," I said.

She went on. "It is hard for me to remember how it actually started. But it did. I met him through a friend at a bar and would see him often. There were the little flirtations here and there, and then somehow we had lunch together and he kissed me and I was his.

Pretty much from that moment on I was his. It was like he knew what buttons to push."

"At first I would take rides in his car at lunch and park in a cemetery and he would get me off with his hand and then I would suck him. Then sometimes we would bring a blanket and we would have sex on the lawn, and every once in a great while I would fuck him at my apartment. This stressed me out greatly but I wanted to please him and he would not bring me to his place. That might put him at risk."

I was already bored with this story. I wished I had some way to distract her from it. That was the thing about ghostwriting. No matter fucking what, you have to roll with it. People pay you to do all sorts of shit, and all of it you have to pretend is interesting.

I worked with this one guy who was writing his life story about how he got diddled as a kid and then went to Nam and killed a bunch of people that didn't look like him. Then he started a karate school that no one went to. I used to sit in his office at his empty karate school while he told me about his life, and how many people would want to buy his book. Nobody wanted to buy his book.

"At some point I told my boyfriend," Staci said. "I had to. It was too much. Pretending all the time that I still cared when all I thought about was Dylan. My boyfriend was upset of course. Things continued as they were for a short while, then both things stopped. Dylan stopped first, he just stopped one day, and he went away. He stopped texting, or emailing. He was gone. Soon afterwards my boyfriend and I broke up too."

"I met Dylan for breakfast once. You know, to try and see if he wanted me now that I was single. I told him it was over between me and my boyfriend. He was still with his girlfriend and he was clear that he wasn't leaving her. I broke down while we both ate. I cried in a quite ugly way, snorting and shaking. He seemed disgusted. He couldn't wait to leave."

This was all making me a little uncomfortable. I wondered if this was when I was supposed to tell her how unattractive she was. I really couldn't take much more of this shit.

"A few months later I heard from him again. This time I had my own place. He would come over quite often. Then somehow I became his slave. How did this happen? I honestly am not really sure. At first he would just have me kiss his body all over, from his head to his feet. Then he would have me lick his feet and kiss him back up to his cock, which I would suck on until he told me to lick his balls. I did this while he jerked off."

"So that's it? Just like that, you became his slave?"

She shrugged. "He's kind of strong-willed. He pretty much gets people to do whatever he wants."

I thought of the pictures of Summer with the moose hat. I grunted.

Staci continued. "After a while, he rarely had sex with me anymore. He started giving me tasks instead. He would have me write 'Dylan is my master' 1,000 times and leave the letter in my mailbox for him to pick up. He would have me steal things from women that I worked with. He would have me go into their purses and take things and bring it to him."

"Then it was the handcuffs and then it was the leash. He had taken to telling me what to wear and how to do my hair on the days that he would come over. He would just come over at lunch usually. We only had an hour or so. That way he would know that he would not have to stay too long. I loved laying with him afterwards but as time went on he would stay just for a few moments and then leave."

"He would put a leash on me and I would bow and kiss his feet. Then he would walk me on all fours around my apartment. I called him master. Always. I still do."

She told this story in an awkward way, like she was telling a story of how she spelled a word wrong in the third grade spelling bee. I couldn't tell if I was getting turned on or repulsed.

"He would tell me how lucky I was to have him. And it was true. I *was* lucky to have him. I was pathetic. I never knew how easy it was to be a slave, to be someone's dog. He would use me as a table. He would put an ashtray on my back and put his feet up on me and smoke, giving my ass an occasional slap. He likes to do that."

"Do what?" I said.

"Slap asses."

Funny. He and I had that in common.

"Anyway, when he came out here he brought me with him. He really doesn't have sex with me at all anymore. I do things to him but he never has sex with me. He does still fuck Rita from time to time."

"Who is Rita?" I said.

"You will meet her today. Rita is prettier than me."

I looked at her. I figured now was the time. "Well I fucking hope so. You are extremely unattractive."

Staci pulled the car over to the side of the road and unzipped my fly.

CHAPTER TEN

I probably should have just stopped her.

Instead, after about five minutes, I came in her mouth. As soon as I did, Staci started up the car and continued driving, but she didn't say another word.

For a moment I had some guilt. I thought of my girlfriend at home missing me, while a rich lunatic's slave was sucking me on the side of the road. I got it though. I really did.

Ghostwriting. Method acting. You have to go all the way into the character. As much as I didn't enjoy my conversation with Staci, I knew more about who Dylan was. He was even more warped than I imagined.

We pulled into a long driveway that led to a rather small house sitting by itself on a cliff above the ocean. We walked inside with Staci carrying my bag. When I entered it looked just like one would expect a house in a suburb to look, it didn't look at all like the house of a rich man, or the house of a Samoan. Whatever the hell that looked like. I still don't know. The whole time I was in Samoa I barely left his house.

I noticed two things right away. The first thing I noticed was Dylan. He was a bit overweight, but in the way that only a certain kind of handsome men can pull off. Kind of like a fat Baldwin brother. He had wild hair that was sticking up all over and he was smiling. The first thing out of his mouth was: "What's up Gorehound?"

The second thing I noticed was a beautiful woman with black hair and dark eyes, who I presumed to be Rita. She was standing frozen and naked towards the side of the room. Her expression was blank. She could almost, but not quite, be a mannequin. She was wearing a blue cowboy hat that was too small for her, and her arms were outstretched in front of her. Her pretty eyes blinked once.

"Hey man," I said to Dylan. "Nice to meet you."

"Woo!" Dylan said. "You made it. Please place your backpack on Rita."

This already didn't seem that odd. I went over and put my backpack over her arms. She didn't move.

As for Dylan, I had sort of expected something different. That he would be 7 feet tall maybe. That he used trees for toothpicks. That he would see me and give me an airplane spin as soon as he saw me. Like the dude couldn't even be real after we had talked. But he was.

"How was your trip?" he said.

"Long."

"Did you get the pics?"

"Of Summer Starr?"

He nodded. "Uh-huh."

"Yeah. Do you want to see them?"

Now he shook his head. "No. They're for you."

I stared at him.

"So this is how it will go," he said. "We are going to stay here for a week or so, or maybe three. Staci will be with you, pretty much all the time. Do what you want to her, or don't. But if you do things to her I am hopeful that will get you more into my mindset. If she is bugging you or something, just tell her to sit in a chair, or go to sleep, face the wall, whatever. You can even put her in her stall. I built one out back for her. It's like a little horse stall for bad girls."

I was tired. I'd been traveling for 24 hours. At this point I was fine with anything. "Whatever you say man, I'm just psyched to be here."

He went on: "Look dude, this book thing with you is going to blow people's minds. You are going to be rich, Dilly. This is a best seller. I spent years being told I had a problem, that I was sick, that I was fucked up, so I came out here to get better, you know? I wanted to get better. I brought Staci and Rita out here with me, of course. You met Staci already, so you know her deal. Rita here is a little different. She used to live in Chicago, made a lot of money in options trading. You know the Chicago Board of Trade? She was a high-powered young business lady. Ambitious. Going places. All that good shit. I met her online. Rita, quack like a duck."

Rita quacked a few times then went back to being frozen.

"Rita and I are doing an experiment. We usually come in and out of shit, but right now, for the whole time you are here she is just going to be my mindless slave. We have been hanging out for years now, and she is pretty cool but you aren't going to get to talk to her at all. She likes country music, and she is conservative politically, so you probably wouldn't enjoy talking to her much anyway. I sure as hell get bored with it pretty quickly."

"Conservative, huh?" I said. I watched her. She didn't look at me. She just stared straight ahead. Her arms must have been getting tired, sticking out like that. She had an amazing body. "She looks sort of Hispanic to me."

Dylan clapped his hands and smiled. "She is! She's a Mexican conservative. Can you imagine? Rita would build the fucking Berlin Wall across Texas to keep her own people out of the country. Well, not this country, not, you know, Samoa. That other one. The US of A. I think you hear me screaming. Anyway, she's the ultimate dittohead. If I let her, she'd tune in to Rush Limbaugh on the internet every single day. But I can't listen to that crap. Rita, say ditto."

"Ditto," Rita said. The movement of her red lips stirred something inside me.

Dylan went on. "Never mind all that. I've kind of wanted to go full bore into the slavery thing with her for a bit anyway. So that's what she and I are going to do. Your thing is going to be to live like me, just a little, listen to me talk, then I am going to do a shitload of drugs and we are going to find the Gods again."

I nodded. "Dylan, I'm fine with that, but I think we should work some things out. How do you even want to go about this? Logistically I mean. How are we going to find the Gods? Do they even do vision quests in Samoa? I thought that was just Native Americans."

He laughed. "Oh, they do them. I use this guy named Afasa for vision quests, although I call him Jerry. It's simpler that way for us both. He also does guided tours if you want one. And he sells weed. He has this shit called White Castle that will fucking blow your mind. I had some brownies the other day and I couldn't get off the floor. You like that? Doing drugs to the extent that you can't get off the floor?"

"Yes," I said, and I meant it. I liked it. Who doesn't?

"Besides, I just told you how we're going to go about it. I am going to tell you stories. While I do this Rita will be a coffee table, or maybe a robot, or maybe she will walk around like a zombie. Staci will be yours. Please insult her as much as you possibly can. It makes her feel comfortable. I will be drunk, or high, or drunk and high, the entire time. I will talk to you of my life, of what I have done, of where I have been. You will listen and write things down. Then we do the real drugs and we find the Gods."

"Dylan, I don't get the connection."

"You will. See, I have some odd habits, with booze, with drugs, and particularly with sex. I went to three different rehabs to try and fix myself. My father threatened to cut me off. I did nothing but get fucked up and cheat on people, and I have a ton of fetishes that people consider bizarre. So to get away from the judgment I came here. I came here with the only two women that tell me there isn't anything wrong with me. But there is. I mean, I know there fucking is. Are you kidding me? And there's something wrong with them, too. The fact that they tell me I'm okay even as I do this shit to them is fucking crazy. Right? Dilly, isn't it fucking crazy?"

"I don't know if I feel comfortable making that judgment yet," I said.

"Of course you don't. Because you're crazy too. You didn't even have to tell me that you drugged a porn star, stripped her naked and put a moose hat on her, because I already knew you did. What the fuck is wrong with you?"

I felt a bit stupid all of a sudden.

"Right? So listen. I came out here where I can keep my fucking money and I can do what I want. I go out to the local bar and I drink like fucking crazy, I smoke tons of weed and I do a shitload of coke. People like me out here. They like me because I'm a big drunk American with lots of money. When I go out to bars I buy the people drinks and make laughing sounds like AHAHAHAHAHHAHAHAA! Rita is my slave, and Staci is too of course. I'm just not really that into Staci much. She isn't that hot."

Staci's neck turned red at this and she let out a tiny little moan. She was becoming hotter to me by the second. I was warming up to the idea that she was going to be mine for a little while.

"So I was doing all that, but the whole time I'm thinking there has to be something more. I mean there fucking has to be, right? It's great doing coke and sitting around trying to see how many things I can find in the house that I can put into Rita's ass. It's great! But that can't be all there is. Listen, here's a fact. Currently there are 33 things in the house that I know of, which I can fit up there. And I haven't given up yet. I'm still looking. But I get tired of that kind of thing. It's stupid. There has to be something more. Then one night I was at the bar and I met Afasa. He's an important guy. He's one of these connectors you read about, knows everybody, has his fat little fingers in everywhere. He told me about this secret vision quest that the locals do, which they don't let outsiders attend."

Dylan suddenly put his hands up, as if to say STOP. "By the way, dude. They also do an awesome traditional barbeque for tourists. It's the same people, but this is a different thing. The vision quest, you know, closed to the public. But the barbecue is for anyone. You have to try it. It's really good." He nodded to himself. "It's so fucking good! I'll tell you, the food alone is worth the trip out here."

I stared at him. "Okay. Barbecue."

"Yeah," he said. "Samoan barbecue, on the beach. Do not miss it. You'll be really fucking sorry you did. Anyway, I went and talked with the head guy, the big chief, the one that does the vision quests. He also makes some amazing mango spiced chicken. He knew my heart was in the right place, so he decided I could go on the quest. I also gave him a shitload of weed and I think that helped his decision."

"So I fasted for four days, and I spent hours in a sweat lodge. Then they came in the middle of the night with a pick-up truck, blindfolded me and drove me to the top of this sacred mountain where they'd had these vision quests for a thousand years. I think they said a thousand but honestly it may only have been a couple of weeks. I was wasted. I also can't remember for sure if it was a sacred mountain or a tainted fountain. But I do remember it was serious fucking business. They left me standing in a little seven-foot circle with a blanket and only a tiny knife to fight off cougars, mountain lions, rattlesnakes, scorpions and whatever else was there. I really don't know what the fuck will kill you out here. I don't go outside much. Bears? Are there bears here? It was so hot it felt like 150 degrees. I thought I was dying."

"I had 12 ounces of water to last me 24 hours. I watched the mountain all day, wondering what they meant by the visions. I found out soon enough. What happens is the shadows change and they talk to you, and when you ask questions you get answers. So that started happening. Then at night I got tired of standing and I lay down on this little blanket. I was really frightened. The coyotes were howling and the place was full of rattlesnakes, and I spoke out loud and said, 'God I'm scared, be with me.' And at that point the mountain range that was above me became the perfect shape of a man lying on his back beside me.

"All the fear left my body and I lay there thinking, 'This is really happening. I'm actually seeing God. I'm so lucky.' And I wasn't scared anymore. Later, the moon came up and changed the shadows and the face turned and was smiling at me, and I was just in complete bliss. I was as light as a feather. And God looked sort of like Uncle Jesse from the Dukes of Hazard, except He was black."

"So all of a sudden I rolled over and I touched Him. It just was for a second and then everything changed. It was at that point that I fucked Him. Although it felt like I was fucking a woman. Maybe He changed into a woman. I don't know. I did it from behind, but it wasn't like I was going to brown town, or, you know, going in through the out door."

I raised my hand. "I get it."

He pointed at me. "Not yet you don't. But you're going to experience it, too. The same as I did."

"I'll do it," I said. "But where does the raping part come in?"

"Oh." Dylan shrugged. "He said no. But I had already started.

CHAPTER ELEVEN

Dylan had Staci show me to my room. I needed a little break. I had been going for way too long. It had started with the moose hat and hadn't stopped.

The room was a nice space with a big comfy bed. There was a window with a warm breeze blowing in. I was happy to finally be able to spend some time by myself, to relax a bit, to be alone.

Except Staci didn't leave. She sat down in a chair and stared at me. She didn't say a word. Neither did I.

Eventually, I went in to take a shower. She came in and washed me. Awkwardly, like a fawn. Then she dried me with a towel and sat back down on her chair. I looked over on the nightstand and saw a bottle that had "chloroform" printed on it in huge letters. Underneath that was an arrow pointing to where Staci was sitting. I looked at her. She nodded slightly. I poured some on a rag, went over and held it to her face. She didn't resist. In fact she breathed it deeply. She went limp right in the chair. Then I went to sleep on the bed.

The next morning I woke up and headed out to the living room with Staci close behind. I felt somewhat refreshed. Dylan was having coffee and had his feet up on the coffee table, which happened to be Rita, naked on all fours.

"Morning!" said Dylan. "I hope you slept okay. Sorry about Staci, I know she is horrifically unattractive. Staci, bring Joey some coffee. Let's start the tape recorder. I want to tell a story about how I lived before I got my trust fund when I was 25."

Staci brought me a cup of coffee blushing like crazy. She looked gorgeous. Rita didn't move an inch. I pressed play on the tape recorder.

He started talking: "I remember back when I was young. I had to work for a bit because I didn't get my trust until I turned 25. Working was supposed to show me modesty, and you know, the value of… what? The value of working, I suppose. My father thought it would help me to know how the rest of you retards lived. Dur, dur, dur. That's you and the rest of the poor people, you sound like that. It was tedious as hell. But when the day was over, I was always out in the bars. I had money for smokes. I would get lunch out every day."

"Then I got married to this woman who loved me and was trying to help me, if you can believe it. She worried about me and all of my boozing and bad habits. We made an agreement. I would sign my check over to her and she would give me 30 bucks. Then we would go to the store and we would shop for lunches. I'd get apples, and sometimes I'd get those little crackers with peanut butter too. I worked right downtown, there were all sorts of places I would have loved to go for lunch, but instead I would sit in the lunch room, eating a fucking apple and wearing the chinos that my wife brought home on sale from Old Navy. This was supposed to teach me to be a man, right? None of the Westerburgers fortune for me."

"The thing is I am irresponsible, I don't pay my bills and I needed help managing things. We needed to save for the future, for kids, to make that extra mortgage payment. What if the trust never came through? My dad is a fucking dick you know, and what if a rogue elephant killed him? Did I really know for sure I was going to get a shit ton of money? She was helping me. When she met me she saved me. See, because I was such a mess."

"That's what she said, of course. I didn't give a fuck about any of that shit."

"But somehow, this had become my life. We both came home from work around the same time, one of us would let out the dog and then she would start to vacuum. She did it every day. Then she'd make dinner and we'd have a glass of wine and watch the TV and get high. I grew my own weed because I couldn't afford to buy it anymore."

"At some point I would want to watch the Celtics or the Red Sox so I'd start rubbing her feet. If she had a glass of wine and got nice and high usually she would pass out within 20 minutes or so when I was giving her a foot massage. Then I could switch the TV to the Celtics. Sometimes if she was really out I'd keep rubbing and masturbate my dick with her feet. She never woke up. Not once."

"We'd fuck about once a month, and when we did it was like fucking the mattress. She just closed her eyes and sprawled on her back and didn't move. She never went down on me the whole time we were together. It was like the thought of taking my dick and putting it in her mouth wasn't appealing to her."

"She'd go away two nights a week for work. That's the other thing – she worked in public relations for a big insurance company."

I checked to make sure my tape recorder was still on, and made a serious face so he could tell I was taking it all in. I was wondering where he was going with all of this.

He continued. "One would think that I could go out when she was away and party my ass off and shit like that. Not on 30 bucks a week. I would hit happy hour at this one bar that had 3 dollar well drinks from 5 to 7. If I drank real fast I could get a good buzz on before I had to go home. It was the same bar that I used to go to all the time when I was single. I knew tons of people there and it was a good time."

"The truth is I get along well in bars. Chicks dig me. I lay back and flirt but I don't make them nervous. I also am ridiculously good looking. In fact I was thinking of calling my book something along these lines: I Am a Ridiculously Good Looking Guy That Wallpapered God's Closet."

At this, he put on a pair of glasses, perched them on the end of his nose and looked down at me.

I shook my head. "No. No good."

He took off the glasses and went on. "So one day my wife has two friends come over, Leah and Patty. She hasn't seen them in a long time and they are coming to go for a dog walk at the park nearby. They both just smile a lot. They remind me of a couple dogs that are constantly wagging their tails. Have you ever seen that? A dog wag its tail? It's funny as shit, Jerry. Every time I see them they look at me and smile, like they really want me to like them or something. "

"So they leave and I am left alone. Both of their purses are sitting on the couch. I unzip the first one. It's Leah's. She has a bunch of credit cards in the pockets, and a Starbucks card. I take that. I check for cash, and she has like 73 bucks. I take 25 and put her wallet back. Then I check out Patty's. Patty has like 130 bucks in her wallet, so I take 40. Then I watch TV. It was Friend Zone on MTV. I fucking loved that show."

"After a while they come back. They hang out for a while then they leave. I take my wife into the bedroom and I fuck her like crazy. I mean, I fucked the shit out of her. I think she dug it. The whole experience made me horny as hell. Probably the same way you felt when you were banging that old rooster moocher Summer Starr. I still can't believe you fucked her like hundreds of times. That's awesome Dilly."

I ignored the part about Summer. "All right," I said. "So you stole money from your wife's friends and got so turned on by that that you fucked your wife? Who you didn't normally like to fuck?"

I was making sure I was getting this.

"Exactly. The next week was awesome. I went to Starbucks every day. A couple days I went out for lunch at work. On the two days that my wife was gone I stayed past happy hour and really flirted a lot with different chicks I knew. I also ate there one night. I had the steak and cheese sliders with fries. They were awesome. I even bought a couple drinks for some other people that I knew. The coolest part was the turn-on lasted all week, buying drinks with those chicks' money. I thought spending my dad's money was great, but this was way better."

"After a week or so, I was broke all over again and it was back to shopping at the supermarket, having lunch in the break room and leaving after a couple drinks at happy hour the nights my wife was away."

"The week after that I was sitting in the bar next to this girl Mia who was there with her boyfriend. Mia was this half-black chick with a big ass. Total dummy, she was always talking about hanging out at home, drinking wine and watching her shows. Mia liked to drink, her boyfriend didn't. She also liked to flirt. So she is sitting there leaning on me and talking to every dude in the place, as her boyfriend gets more and more pissed off. She is to my left at the bar, while her dude sits to her left. I notice her wallet is sticking out of her coat pocket right next to me. I take it. There wasn't any forethought involved. I just did it. I pulled it out of her pocket and stuck it in my coat pocket. I went out for a smoke and rifled through it. Twelve fucking bucks. I tossed it in a trashcan and went back inside."

"Now I won't say I didn't feel a rush. I did. WOOOOOOOOO! My heart was pounding and I felt like it was going to beat out of my fucking chest. I also can't say I didn't like it. I did. I really liked it."

"So I get to have a couple more drinks. I also get to enjoy Mia looking all over for her wallet. She looked everywhere and the more she looked the more her cuckolded boyfriend got pissed off at her. Me and the bartender, who is a chick named Eileen, kept kind of rolling our eyes about it, how funny it was and all of that. Eileen couldn't stand Mia."

"So then the next week I was talking to this chick named Suzanne that hung out there all the time. I mean like ALL the time. She worked in advertising and was a total boozebag, there is no doubt about it. She was one of those chicks that hears people say funny things in bars and then puts what they say in quotation marks on Facebook."

"Gross," I said.

Dylan nodded. "Right? I mean, come on. So as always she was getting trashed. She had her purse on the back of her chair, kind of like one of those big purses that you can fit all sorts of stuff in. She was going on and on about nothing and was totally hammered. As a matter of fact, we went out for a smoke at one point and I slapped her on the ass. She just stood there like a statue with a drunk smile pasted on her face. I was doing that for a while, making ass slaps my patented move. It is amazing how many asses you can slap if you do it just at the right place, and the right moment. Anyway, so on the way out I kind of stood behind her for a bit and lifted her wallet and left. I checked it out in the car. There was 170 bucks in it."

"My wife was back the next night. I bought her a card with Suzanne's money about how much I loved her, and I fucked the hell out of her again. After she vacuumed up the place, of course."

"The next week was awesome. I bought a couple of used books to read and went out to lunch three different days. I had a really awesome steak burrito one time. The meat had an awesome sear on it. When my wife took off for a few nights for work, I went back to the bar and stayed until last call. Eileen was bartending and although it was busy for a while, later on it got slow as fuck. At one point she went out for a smoke, and I saw her purse behind the bar. Actually I had been looking at it all night. It was on a part of the bar where I could reach over and go through it without going back there. There were a few people down the bar a ways and a couple booths were full, but no one was nearby. I reached over and found her wallet, grabbed some cash out of it and put it in my pocket. No one noticed. She came back in and started talking to me. In fact we pretty much rapped the rest of the night. At one point I went into the bathroom and checked out my haul. It was about 80 bucks."

"I came back out and Eileen was talking to this other chick Marie who bartends at another bar I used to go to sometimes. I always kind of wanted to bang her but she seemed crazy. Like you wake up and she is standing next to your bed with a knife crazy. Anyway, they are going somewhere when Eileen gets off and I decide I am going too."

"We go to a party. Well, if you call 12 people doing coke and getting drunk a party, which I do. I start working Marie, not because I wanted to fuck her but because it is fun to do. The energy is there, I can sense it, I tell her stories about my controlling, vacuuming wife. I leave out the part about beating off with her passed out feet. Marie understands how difficult it is for me. She really does. While Marie is going through her purse to get a smoke I see a shitload of cash just floating around in there."

"I mention it, joking of course, like, 'Whoa, you are loaded.' She just laughs and tells me that as a bartender she hardly ever goes to the bank, she just throws cash in her purse. I think at this point about just hitting her over the head with a lamp, taking her purse and going on the run, but then I remember that I am going to be totally fucking rich one day. So instead I just sort of subtly laugh like: hehehehehehehe."

"At one point everyone is partying in the kitchen. There are maybe 6 of us left. Everyone else took off. This one girl that I know a little named Melissa is passed out on the couch in the living room. You have to go right by her to get to the bathroom. Her purse is on the floor next to the couch. Melissa is a bartender too. My third trip to the bathroom I grab her purse and bring it into the bathroom with me. There is like 300 bucks in it."

"The next few weeks were amazing. It is like I found the secret of life. Stealing! Honestly if you find shit around here and steal it who could blame you? Not me. If I invite you here, and you fuck my women and take my money, who is the one at fault? There are no victims, Joey. Just volunteers. Anyway, I was living fat. I bought a new Kanye CD I had been wanting forever and went out to lunch every day. My foot rubs had become more involved and joyous and my wife spent more time unconscious on the couch while I watched TV. I started banging her at least once a week. She starts telling me she loves me much more often and when she vacuums she sings and hums."

"When my wife goes away I hit the bar each night and stayed until last call. I started taking a few more days off from work but that was cool, I had plenty of vacation time. Marie and I were flirting a lot. I can tell I confuse her, and a confused girl is as good as mine. Confusion is the entire key to getting laid."

I didn't say anything. I glanced at the recorder. It was still rolling.

He went on. "So anyway, I want the money in Marie's bag, but she always puts the bag on the floor, or in her lap. One night, as we have a smoke we start to kiss. Her bag is on her shoulder. I reach in and feel a bunch of bills. I pull the wad out and put the bills in my pocket. When I go to the bathroom later it is only like 23 dollars in fives and ones."

"She starts to text me all the time. Often now after my wife falls asleep beside me I spend my time texting Marie back instead of watching the Celtics or beating off with my wife's feet. It seems that now in Marie's mind we are having an affair, while in my mind I cannot stop thinking about all that cash in her bag. Her cash is the most important thing to me in the world. I want it, all of it. The money she has isn't even money anymore. It is something way more than that. That purse has become something I orbit around. When she buys drinks I can see it. Sometimes she pulls out her wallet and it is thick with bills, other times I can just see them floating around inside of it."

"One night it happens. My wife is gone and Marie is drunk. I take her to my place. We get in bed and we kiss, she starts playing with my cock. At first I just try and cuddle her so she will pass out, but she keeps talking. All this talking she's doing is keeping her awake. Finally she goes down on me. She is holding herself up with one arm and is so drunk she keeps sort of losing purchase, her head keeps falling off my cock and banging into the bed."

"I realize there is only one thing to do. I fuck the hell out of her. I start standing up beside the bed with her feet around my ears, and then I flip her over and do her from behind. Then I go down on her and finish up with a straight up missionary type scene. Woooooo! She had to have cum about five times. I haven't though, so I decide to fake it. I figure with the amount of booze and orgasms she's had she will be asleep pretty much as soon as I pull out."

"So I do it. I groan and spasm a little and pull out and within like a minute she is making some sort of snore/wheeze combination that lets me know she is done for the night. Just to make sure I give her ass a few little slaps, but her breathing and cadence don't change."

"This is possibly the most exciting moment of my entire life. I get out of bed and pick up her purse, which is sitting on the floor. I honestly cannot even believe it. There is like a grand in there. There is probably 500 in the wallet and another 500 just lying around in loose bills. I take like 100 and get back in bed. I can't sleep, so I get up and pick up her purse again. This time I turn on the light and put her purse on her stomach. It rises and falls as she breathes. The snoring continues. Fuck it. I take all of it. I count it and it's like 1100 bucks."

"Of course I will have to find another bar to go to. I can never go there again. But I think of the all the months of lunches out, and of drinking out when my wife is away. Eleven hundred bucks would last me two months, maybe three. Three months! And every time I buy a fucking hot dog from the weird guy in the park, or go down to Old Orchard Beach and eat French fries it will be because of this moment right now."

"Finally, I fall asleep. When I wake up, Marie is walking around the bedroom that I share with my wife. She is looking for her purse. It is around 6 in the morning. She sees it and picks it up. Then she sees me looking at her. 'Come here, babe,' I say. She smiles and comes over to me and we kiss."

Dylan stopped talking. When he did, it was like a spell was broken. He sat there and stared at me. I stared back, confused.

"Look at you," he said. "What the fuck is up with you? I seriously can't tell. If I were gay you would confuse me and then I would suck your dick."

"Let me ask you a question," I said. "You want all this in the book?"

He shrugged. "Yeah. Why?"

"Well, you're a rich guy, stealing money from women who are supposed to be your friends, or that you sleep with. It makes you seem like an asshole."

He laughed. "I guess you don't really get it yet. I am an asshole. Right after that, I finally got my trust fund, and I left my wife for Rita here. This book is ABOUT me being an asshole. It is about me being an asshole, then going on a vision quest and meeting the Gods. By the way, just so you know, you're an asshole too. You're just more afraid than I am."

"Okay," I said. "All right if we take a break?"

"That's a good idea," he said. He waved his hand, as if dismissing me. "Break away. You're gonna need your rest. The shit I want to talk about this afternoon will make your brain explode."

CHAPTER TWELVE

I went into my room to relax for a bit. I got on my laptop while Staci crouched on the floor and kissed the soles of my feet. I didn't even really notice. I was getting used to this method-acting thing.

I checked my email. There was one from my girlfriend, of course. She was worried about me. She thought I was dead. She probably would have called my mom except she hadn't met my parents. All of a sudden I realized my kindly, silver-haired, aging parents didn't know where I was either.

I was a dick. Here I was in Samoa, having this awkwardly hot chick kiss my feet and listening to a lunatic rant. All for 5,000 bucks. Of course I was hoping there would be more money, but maybe there wouldn't. That thought gave me a sinking feeling. Dylan was a fucking maniac. I might never see another dime from him. I started to wonder if it was a mistake to come out here.

I didn't write my girlfriend back. It was for the best anyway. I mean, what the fuck? I am 20 years older than her, and I am crazy. I also still miss my ex-wife. I miss having conversations. I miss laughing. There is something about getting older where you don't even care as much anymore that things won't work out. You know they won't and that is okay. I sort of want things to not work out anymore. I want to be alone in a room, with a shitty laptop. I don't want a slave, and I don't want some hot young chick smiling at me.

My next email was from a dominatrix who wanted to write a book with me:

...

December 25

3:30 AM

Brian.

Thank you for getting in touch. I have had the idea for quite some time to write a book. I wrote down a lot of what I have done. And lucky or unlucky for me a lot of the things I have seen and done are forever etched in my mind. It's like some sort of PTSD, equipped with flashbacks of assholes. I mean actual assholes, not jerky men.

It was great speaking with you. I want to talk about it more. I am interested in working with you. You have a good attitude and the other writers I have spoken with have a lot going on, so I felt like I wouldn't really be a priority for them. You seem to have plenty of time. I'm super motivated, hard working and not one to give up when faced with obstacles. As my profile as a Dom has risen over the past year, I have been approached by the UK fashion magazine Barron. They're going to run an article on me. Also, a guy from Vogue is coming to do a photo shoot. Exciting stuff.

I really think that sharing my experiences would be great exposure for me on many levels. I have a unique perspective as I'm super grounded, down to earth and sober :D That's pretty unusual for a Dominatrix. It will be like a memoir of a sane person in an insane asylum. Boy, do I have some crazy stories.

The first Mistress I worked with I met through a man I was experimenting with. My role in the relationship was as the submissive. He is another story, but I'd like to tell you a little about my introduction into the Dominatrix profession.

As instructed by my master, I called Mistress Corrine, and made my way to her dungeon. It was located in the seedier side of Silver Lake, Los Angeles. It was a Mexican neighborhood, metal fences wrapped neatly around the small apartment complexes, keeping the dogs and children out of the street.

Once I had parked, I let myself in through the gate, walked past a blind old lady who must have lived in the downstairs apartment, and came to the front door. I was greeted by a middle-aged, normal looking guy, who ushered me up the steep, dark staircase, lined with tacky fetish and erotic art. The dungeon was small but quite nicely decorated in white and a tasteful shade of forest green. Chains hung from the wall in the shape of a cross, a fair sized leather bondage table was pushed into the corner opposite a cleverly placed mirror.

My first impressions were good.

A tall, thin, blonde lady greeted me with a smile and a hug. She was Mistress Corrine. She invited me into the next room. It was a usual bedroom type setup, bed, TV, closet with a table and chairs. We talked for about 20 minutes about my experience and availability. At the time I thought nothing of the large glass of white wine she was nursing (it was 11am), or the fact that she had a lot of bruises on her arms. I happily agreed to come in for my initial training.

A few nights later I arrived promptly, my make-up and hair perfect, stockings, garter and a sexy thong and bra set concealed under my dress. To look at me no one would ever have guessed what I would be up to that evening. Not even me.

I was met by the same middle-aged man, who took me up to the dungeon where I was greeted by Mistress Corrine again, and another of her slaves – a young, fairly good looking Indian guy. Mistress Corinne was dressed in a short, cheap looking PVC micro dress with nothing on underneath. I could clearly see her shaven pussy peeking out as she raised her hand to drag from her cigarette and her glass of wine. I slipped off my dress as Mistress Corrine instructed the slaves to get on their backs on the bondage table. She handed me a tub of slimy lube along with elbow length latex gloves.

As I pulled the gloves on, the slaves took turns inhaling poppers. The smell was intoxicating and I could already feel my head spinning slightly.

"This is how you do fisting," Mistress Corrine said. She was already up to her elbow in the Indian slave's ass. It was like her arm was being swallowed up. I lubed up my hand and started working my four fingers into the asshole that lay before me.

"It's okay, he can take it," she told me. "He's been in prison for the past ten years and just got out." More and more of my hand, wrist and then arm was engulfed. I had only slipped a finger or two into a boyfriend's ass while in college – and my boyfriend was tight. This was a totally new experience. I began rhythmically pumping my arm in and out of the slave. He took it so easily. I couldn't believe what I was doing!!!

There is so much to tell. From my first shit eater to the crazy drug addicted mistresses, A-list celebrity clients, and all the etc…

I'm sure I can tell a compelling story that people will not be able to stop reading.

I'm available to Skype or chat more anytime. My real name is Theresa but people call me Maxi.

. . .

I stopped reading. I heard myself sigh heavily. I sounded like a tire with the air leaking out of me. I felt that way, too. This was my life. Nothing but crazy people as far as the eye could see.

I looked down at Staci who was still dutifully kissing the bottom of my feet.

"Hey babe, can you stop doing that for a bit? I have to write an email."

CHAPTER THIRTEEN

Later, when I came out of my room, Rita was on a leash, on all fours, with a rubber dog toy in her mouth. Dylan was patting her ass. Every time he tapped her ass, the toy squeaked.

"Hey man," he said. "Are you ready? I want to talk about rehab today. This is the shit that's going to blow your mind."

"It's your book," I said. "Let me get set up and we can start."

I started my tape recorder and sat down. Sometimes I just pretend to tape record things. Especially on the phone. I will be like, "Hang on one second. I need to get this started." It makes people think I am paying attention. I don't need to hear every word someone says to ghostwrite. But with Dylan I had the feeling I did.

"Okay, all set. Go."

"All right," he said. "Here I go. I am going… right now. As I told you before, a few years ago, before I came out here, I was threatened by my father with a loss of income if I didn't go to treatment for my sex problems. So I did. I went to fucking treatment."

"First of all I don't like the term sex addict. It has a connotation that I don't enjoy. But I had to go, or I was going to be cut off. No thanks. It's been a long time since I've had a job. You dig?"

"I dig," I replied, and I did.

"Right. At first, I didn't want to do inpatient. The thought of being locked up with 20 other guys like me for a month sounded like hell. So I chose a place in LA that did intensive outpatient programming. Basically I would stay in a hotel for two weeks, go to groups and do individual counseling all day, go to Sex Addicts Anonymous meetings at night, and after two weeks I would come home cured. But it didn't work, that's what the counselors said, so it was off to Philadelphia for a month of inpatient."

"Exactly what I didn't want. It was like a jail for freaks. It might be helpful for me to talk a bit about the people I was in there with. Do you want to hear about that?"

"Yeah man," I said. "Of course I do." I didn't, though. I didn't want to hear about it. I'd only been here a day, and already I was tired. I didn't want to listen to him anymore. I didn't want to hear stories about him stealing. I didn't want to hear about all of the weird people he knew. I was even getting tired of looking at Rita be a coffee table. She wasn't beautiful anymore. She was becoming something else instead.

He packed a bowl with marijuana, lit it and took a bit hit. He offered it to me. I declined. He set the bowl and the lighter on Rita's back.

"All right. Let's start with Reed. Reed wasn't an addict. He was engaged to this chick, she had bit tits and was rich, so he didn't want to lose her. She caught him cheating so he pretended he had a problem. He also used to go to clubs a lot, to see chicks dance and shake their tits in his face. That was kind of his whole scene. He was a cool guy, really mellow, kind of funny. He knew he wasn't supposed to be there. I kept in touch with him for a while, but not for long. Who wants to be reminded of shit like this?"

"Then there was Al. Al was a doctor. He had affairs. He got fired from jobs for sexual harassment. He didn't think he was fucked up. He thought his scene was normal. He didn't fit in with the rest of us at all. You know, the rest of us were cool. One time we went to Johnny Rockets though. That's pretty dorky, but I had never been there before."

He looked at me for a few seconds until I nodded, then he continued on.

"Gary was different from Al. Gary knew he was fucked up. His thing was just banging random dudes. He banged thousands of them over time. Like that sounds fake – thousands – but he totally did. THOUSANDS of people! Can you imagine that shit? Mostly they were young, and almost always they were prostitutes. Most of the time he would pick them up, fuck them in a motel room, pay them, and leave. He lived out in LA where it was kind of easy to find some dude to bang that was pretty and needed money. I wouldn't have the first idea where to find something like that. I don't remember much else. He had kind of cool hair and he wasn't a dick. He had a boyfriend that he had lived with for years. He had a trust fund. He got freaked out when it was mentioned to him that looking at kids getting fucked on his computer could lead him to be arrested. So we stopped mentioning it."

"That brings us to Matt. Matt was a dick. He used to go to Thailand a lot and bang tons of underage prostitutes. He was a businessman of sorts. I remember he was engaged at one point and a big part of his thing was about how maybe he could get engaged again. Not how he could stop banging 12-year-old girls, but how he could get back with the love of his life. Not that I can't relate. The heart wants what the heart wants."

"Ben was a married guy in the military. He was a sub. His whole thing was going to Doms and giving them money. I believe dudes like that were called cash pigs. I don't think he would even actually 'go' to them. He would just start relationships online and then they would tell him he was a stupid fuck and then he would give them money and beat off. Being turned on by being an idiot. Such a cool concept."

At that he paused and slapped Rita's ass hard. The dog toy squeaked again. He looked at Staci. "Staci could you take off your clothes and put on your fez?"

"Yes Master," she said.

"Anyway, back to it again. Then there was Marcus. People know this dude, he was kind of well known publicly. He liked to show people his dick, and he was just out of prison for doing so.

93

The dude was huge, black and scary and he loved freaking people out. He played in the NBA for a few years, but it didn't last, then he went and played in the Philippines. The owner of the team paid for his women, but then he partied too much, even for the Philippines. That's heavy partying. So then he was out of basketball and ended up getting busted for sitting around beating off in his truck in his home state. When you're famous, huge and black, you can only beat off in your truck for so long before you get arrested."

"Me and Marcus and this guy Nate were tight. We would hang out outside all night and smoke cigarettes and talk until they made us come back inside. Nate was my roomie and I didn't hate him. That in itself should let you know how much I liked him."

"Nate used to deal crack and be naked. Sometimes he wouldn't put on clothes for weeks and people would come over and buy crack and Nate would just sit there naked dealing it out and sucking on a pipe. I mean, let's face it, that sounds awesome but how long does the story of a happy naked crack dealer last? Not very long. Dealing crack and using it is like a monkey trying to sell bananas. Get it? Nate used to say, 'Dude, I'm allergic to crack … every time I use it I break out in handcuffs.' Funny. He said the monkey thing, too. I tried to make it mine but he said it first."

"So he would hit the pipe and he would hang out in dressing rooms in the mall and just kind of wait until some chick looked up, and there he was naked... hair down to his waist, like a cracked-out Jesus in a Macy's dressing room. Can you imagine Dilly? There he was and of course it was just an accident. Out of the hundreds of times he did this, he only got caught once or twice. He thought some girls liked it. He would tell me so. I liked him, so I'd kind of nod and grunt in agreement but I mean, dude... He'd do this at beaches, too. Like some woman would be walking by his car and hey, there would be Nate, all floaty on crack and changing in his car... by mistake, of course. It happens every day."

"My favorite was when he out driving, he would see some woman out walking. Then he would race ahead of her and get on a stranger's porch – naked, of course – and wait for the woman to walk by. Then he would light his crack pipe. She'd look up and see him there. Godly. Unafraid. Again it was an accident... he was just out on his porch naked, smoking crack. He didn't know someone would happen along. So he went to jail. When I met him he'd just gotten out. For him rehab was all fun and mellow, a break from jail, while for me it was jail."

"We smoked. We smoked so much. God, I loved to smoke. I was so skinny back then. I was living off of bacon and Marlboros. I looked fucking great. WOOO! I would choke down three cigarettes in fifteen minutes and wait two minutes, then smoke three more. We smoked and did the jailhouse stroll around the property. During these walks we lied to each other about how the other one was really not that fucked up. Nate didn't think I should even be there. I mean, I wasn't that messed up. I told Nate that the fact he thought his counselor Holly was in love with him was perfectly normal."

"Nate was the best at role playing. One time this dude Jim was playing Nate's dad and Nate pile-drived him into a chair. Nate hated his dad, I guess. I never played anyone's dad. I only got to play the inner addict. You know, the devil on your shoulder. I was like the bad guy. Even in rehab, I was worried about how cool I would be, about what the other guys would think of me, but believe me I was really cool. They fucking loved me. Anyway, after Nate got out he didn't know where he was going to go, but he did have a hundred grand or so saved up – that's what he said – so he was okay. But about three weeks after he left, his new cell phone went straight to voicemail. A few months after that, his phone was shut off entirely. I have to think he went back to jail, that he broke out in handcuffs again. You see what I did there? Broke out in handcuffs?"

"Yeah man," I said. Ha."

I was starting to space out. What the fuck was this? Now he is going to give me a laundry list of all the fucked up people he knew in rehab and tell me how cool they all thought he was?

He went on. "Mark was another guy. He was always picked to play the woman when we did role plays. He was always the long suffering wife. In reality he fucked with women in a big way. He had come all the way from New Zealand to be cured. Apparently there wasn't anywhere in New Zealand for freaks like us to go. His thing was just lying and manipulating. Most holidays he would spend with his own family and another family as well. Like somehow he would leave his wife and kids on Christmas and go over to some other chick's house he was banging and hang out with her and her kids too. He would always tell the women that fell for him how much he loved them. But he never did love them. Not even a little. I don't think he loved anybody. He was cool enough, but there was something about him that was not quite right. He was a missing a piece of the puzzle."

"Joey was a peeping tom. He would creep around his neighborhood late at night, and peep at people and beat off. I didn't know him that well. I am not sure anyone did. I am sure that his wife didn't and I am sure his co-workers didn't as well. I could tell he thought he was better than everyone else. I thought I was better than everyone else too, so we had that in common."

For some reason, I wanted to punch him. Of all the pointless books I had worked on, this was turning out to be the most pointless. For the last twenty minutes he had been telling me about exhibitionists and peeping toms. He was smiling at me. His feet were up on Rita's naked back.

"Joey was good looking," Dylan said. "He had a cute little haircut. He was married and was a salesman of sorts. Corporate low 6 figure type. He wanted to fuck everyone. I mean like everyone. Your mom, your nephew, your football coach. Everyone."

"The staff at the rehab would give some guys in there a test. It's called an IAT – the implicit association test. It tells you things about yourself, tendencies you might have, that you're maybe not even quite aware of yourself. The one they give in sex rehab is supposed to make some dudes come to terms with the fact that they want to bang kids. So the guys the staff knew wanted to bang kids they would give a test. It's like a stimulus response kind of thing, where they would put this guy in a room and show him photos of a 6-year-old boy and a 25-year-old hot chick until the guy would finally prove to them and himself what everyone else in the world already knew. It would tell them that the guy wanted to fuck kids."

"Then the guy would wander around for days moaning about the fact that the test was wrong, and the staff was wrong and he didn't, he really didn't, want to fuck kids at all. But my point is that Joey wasn't like that. He would just tell you. He wanted to fuck everyone. Like I imagine that if a kid is ugly, or a woman was really fat he wouldn't want to fuck them. No one wants to fuck an ugly kid. But this was his template. If it was a young girl, young boy, adult male, adult female, he didn't really care."

"Imagine walking around in Chucky Cheese and getting off on everyone. I mean everyone. From the chubby teen age girl taking your ticket, to the 6-year-old boy playing skee ball, and then you turn around and look at some mom's fat ass, and then when you are taking a leak you look at the dude's cock next to you. That's a wild ride."

"To make things worse, or better, depending on your perspective, he also liked looking in windows. This was the reason he went to rehab in the first place. He got caught. He would go out at night and go for a jog. Sometimes he would jog when his wife was asleep. He lived in a nice neighborhood in California, the kind of place where a young newly married hero would live."

"He got kind of obsessed with a family down the street. Mom, dad and a 9-year-old boy. He would go most nights and watch them. Not just them, of course. He would check other people out too, but it became them most of the time. He would time his jogs for the son's bedtime and watch the kid take his clothes off and get into bed. Then he would watch the mom and the dad move around the house, watch TV, drink wine, fuck. And Joey would jerk off. I think he liked the dad the most. I think he said that. I can't recall for sure. I do recall that at least once he said he went inside the house and beat off next to the kid's bed."

I raised my hand. Dylan stopped and looked at me.

"You said this guy was a friend of yours?"

He shrugged. "No. I wouldn't say a friend. I was in there with him, though. I guess he was okay, as sex rehab goes."

"All right," I said.

"Anyway, where was I? He said when he went out at night, his body would feel like it was on fire. He used to say it was like an electrical current. His whole body was just charged right the fuck up and he felt so, so high. So at some point he got caught. He didn't get caught in the house, and he didn't get caught beating off, but he did get caught outside someone else's house. Looking in a window with his eyes wild, his heart beating out of his fucking chest, explaining to a cop why he, a six-figured captain of industry, was standing in someone's back yard in the middle of the night. Next to a window. Wearing a running suit. With a cute little haircut. So he went to rehab."

I started rubbing my temples. I wanted to get up and go for a walk. "Anybody else?"

"Yeah, there was this one guy, an obese married dude that was hooked on phone sex. He called 900 numbers. He would run up bills in the thousands. He always acted all cheerful like being in rehab was a fucking blast or something."

"Which reminds me of Jeff. Jeff was the same type. He started a prayer group. I tell you man, if there is anyone in any sort of bad situation and you are trying to judge his character, a good way is to see if he is in prayer group or not. The dude came in with coke dripping out of his nostrils and he hated the place. What a schmuck. He was pleasant at least. But totally fake. If you have ever been to rehab, you know the type. There are a few types in rehab."

"First you have the total fuck ups. They won't do anything. They just sit there. They don't participate. Kind of enough said. Probably makes up about 10 percent. Now I am talking about a rehab you PAY for. Not one you have to go to for court. These guys paid 10 grand to be here for a month, but they don't do a fucking thing."

"Also at 10 percent are the people that really get it. They give themselves over to it, they really mean it. They have had enough and they want to get better."

"Then you have my type. Probably makes up 30 percent. We do try a little. We do assignments, we participate. We want to get better. But we fucking hate it. It blows. We giggle a lot, we form bad boy cliques, and we smoke tons of cigs. We are honest with each other that we will probably always be fucked up."

"Jeff's group probably makes up 50 percent. The fakes. Jeff rolls in on the very first day and hits me up. He hits me up because out of the 15 or so of us I look more normal than most. Jeff looks TOTALLY normal. He is a 40-year-old geek – thin, red hair, glasses. He wears almost nothing but those fucking 'Life is Good' t-shirts the whole time he is there. He works in international investments for Brown Brothers in New York and makes like 1.5 million a year. So this is kind of what he says. 'Fuck this I gotta get out of here. My wife cut off all my money and credit cards. This place fucking sucks. I gotta get out of here.' This continues constantly for like three days until on the fourth day he starts prayer group."

"For the rest of the time there he is so fucking happy he came, it changed his life, between the rehab and prayer group he is a changed person. Just like that. Over night. In reality of course Jeff decided fighting it was pointless and that wifey would take him back and he would have no expensive divorce if he faked it for a little while. He had done all of these horrific things since he was married but the biggest thing he was worried about telling her was that he once banged a dude. Seriously."

"Jeff also liked coke. A lot. So his big thing was he would get a hotel room for a few days, blow a shitload of coke and get some hookers. The thing is that he would never touch the hookers, and the hookers were not allowed to move. His whole trip was 'bringing porn to life.' So the hookers would come in, take their clothes off, pose and not move. If they talked or moved too much he would freak the fuck out, scream at them and kick them out of the room. Then call for another chick. That honestly sounds way more fun than prayer group. Then again, I never went to prayer group."

I shut the recorder off. "Hey man, mind if we take a break for a minute?"

"What?" he said. "Why? This is gold I'm giving you."

It was gold, all right. It was a golden shower. And it was too much. All of it was just too fucking much.

"I don't know. I feel like I need some fresh air."

"Okay, one sec Gorehound, we're almost done. Bill was another one. He was cool. He was there for fucking. He fucked a lot of chicks and he also fucked a lot of dudes. He would bang his wife in the morning, then bang his mistress at lunch, then on the way home on the train from NYC he would bang some random dude in the bathroom at the station. I think he thought this might not be a sustainable lifestyle, so he decided to get some help."

"Sean liked porn and strip clubs. This bored the rest of us greatly. Get a real problem, dude."

"Erik loved poppers and sex clubs. He worked as a nurse all week and then would spend about 14 straight hours barebacking 6 different dudes and doing poppers all the while. He often talked about how much he wanted to leave rehab and just go to a sex club and fuck like 10 dudes."

Finally Dylan stopped talking and looked at me. Rita was still naked on all fours with the squeak toy in her mouth. I noticed Staci was now standing in the room naked and wearing a fez.

"There you go dude," Dylan said. "Make something of that, and make us all likeable. Maybe make it like Oceans 11 or something. I could totally see this as a movie. I was thinking the guy that married

Monica from Friends would play you."

"Am I in the story?" I said.

He smiled. "You're here, aren't you?

CHAPTER FOURTEEN

I got drunk that night. I made my own Vodka tonics and I just kept pouring them stronger and stronger. I went to bed early, tried to fuck Staci, but couldn't get it up. When I woke up in the morning she was in bed with me. She was curled up behind me holding my stomach. I looked at the clock and it was two in the afternoon. I went out to the living room. Dylan was there as always.

Rita stood next to him naked with her arms outstretched in front of her.

"Brian....what the fuck? You slept late. What is up with you?"

I was about to speak, but he waved it away.

"Guess what? I decided to do a zombie slave thing with Rita today. She's just a mindless zombie now. And you know what's odd about that? The longer we do this 24-7, the more I forget that she was ever even real."

I looked at Rita. She didn't look at me or even seem to notice I was there. "Right," I said. "What are we onto today?"

Dylan smiled. "Stories. Ready?"

I fired up the tape recorder. "Go."

"This was when I lived in Portland. Me and my buddies Todd and Mort were heading downtown one night to get drunk when we came across a cop car with its window down and no one in it. We just had to fuck with it. There is honestly no telling what the three of us will do when we are together!"

"We picked up some dog shit that we saw laying nearby and started to put it on the front seat of the cop car. Well, we didn't actually pick it up. None of us wanted to touch it with our hands. So we did it in a way that was quite ingenious and involved several steps. There were three of us and we formed this sort of human conveyer belt, kind of hacky sack thing. Like my buddy would kick the shit from the ground onto my other buddy's shoulder and then he would twitch and it would go to my arm and I would kind of pop and lock until it landed in the car. It really was a fine time for a while but then some people came along and started looking at us."

"Some of them loved it of course, while others wanted us dead. Half of the crowd was laughing and looking out for us. The other half was screaming at us that we were going to jail and who would do such a thing, and that even though we didn't think so, we had dog shit all over us."

"Soon some typical military types decided they were going to play cops for the cops and started charging at us from across the street and telling us to knock it off. Some people on our side starting screaming, 'Drop the dog shit and run! They are going to kill you!" Which honestly seemed possible at the moment, but I tell you, I can totally pull off the crazy vibe. I've been able to get away with it ever since I killed my uncle Stan by peeing in his mouth."

"I've also seen plenty of big dogs get scared by little dogs. So I puffed up and ran right at them. I ran as fast as I could and I screamed the entire way. 'Mind your own fucking business you dicks, it's a fucking joke on the cops!!! It's just a fucking joke and if you come one step closer I am going to drop to my knees and gnaw your fucking dick off!'

"I was hoping this would work. One time I was camping out in the woods near a guy that was in an RV and being really loud. I was just into hanging out and doing nothing in the woods and here this guy was acting like he was hanging out in Oakland. So I went over there to try and chill him out. I banged on the door of his camper, all angry-like, and as soon as he opened the door he just dropped to his knees and started sucking my cock. I tell you it freaked me the fuck out. I didn't bother him for the rest of the night after that. Even now talking about it I still get the willies thinking about that half an hour where that queer was sucking my cock."

"Anyway, there was no way I was actually going to gnaw the dicks off these military guys, but these are the kind of guys that get freaked out by anything all gayed up so they backed right off."

"Once we put as much dog poop as we could all over the car, we turned on the lights and siren, hid in the bushes and waited for the cops to show up. We only lasted for about a minute though because the siren was totally annoying and also everyone kept yelling things like, 'I can see you in the bushes' and 'You've got dog shit all over you.'

"So we bounced. The three of us went on down the road and back to my place. When we got there we started talking about how I had punked those guys with the whole 'I am going to gnaw your dick off' thing and we laughed and laughed. We were starting to have a good time but the only problem was something smelled like shit really bad."

Dylan glanced up at me. "How's that so far?"

I stopped the tape recorder. "You're making this whole thing up," I said.

He looked sheepish, but just for a second. Then he nodded.

"Right. Let's get back to sex. Here's something fucked up that really is true:

CHAPTER FIFTEEN

I hit play on the tape recorder and he began again.

"One of my hobbies is that when I lived in Maine, I used to lie to women on the internet all the time. If I get bored I still do it. Even from here, halfway around the world, I still do it. Now basically, when I say I lie to them what I really mean is that they fall for me. Not all of them. Some blow me right off. Others flirt with me a bit here and there, but then go away. Others flirt hard. Then there are the ones that not only flirt but start talking about how we should get together. There are the ones that want to get together and bang."

He stopped and looked at me. I said nothing so he continued on.

"Then there are the ones that love me. They become obsessed

with me purely because of what I write or what I say. I find that amazing, that people can fall in love with someone they have never met, because of words. It is an incredible fucking turn-on to me when I can do that, when I can make someone mine, and mold them, just through my words."

"How does it happen? What piece of the brain turns on just a few words? You'd think it would be impossible. It isn't. It happens all the time. Way more than you might expect. You think about how empires are built. Some have been built through force, but most have been built by people like me. You see my slaves here. I don't force them into this. They do it because of the way I act and what I say."

"There have been so many over the years. Of course, sooner or later one has to augment it with the text, and then the phone call. But most of the work is done online via the written word."

"Sarah was the first, I think. I mean first to say she loved me. I met her online because we both were writing blogs. I wish I was making this up, but it's true. I would leave comments, then she would, and then we sent messages. It feels so empowering and yet so ridiculous when it happens. I laugh when they say what I want them to say. It is funny as fuck. I usually have to go first. I give her something like: 'I know this might sound odd, but I am really starting to like you.' Oddly enough, she feels the same way. I mean she really likes me too. Who knew?"

"It's not weird. It's wildly romantic. It isn't that we don't know each other. In fact we have spent more time writing and letting each other know things about ourselves than most people who have been out on a lot of dates. So then that's it. We love each other. Yay! By then we are texting and talking constantly on the phone and making plans to meet. Which is a huge fucking pain in the ass, and not really what I'm in it for. So I bailed on Sarah at this point. Sarah is shattered, and I'm just glad I don't have to talk to her anymore."

"So then I move on to Jane. Jane is a multi-pierced, tattooed chick that lives in Australia. She blogs as well. In fact, she knows Sarah as an online friend. Jane and I discuss how simple Sarah was to take things the wrong way and to go that far with it in an online relationship. I mean it was basically totally fucking stupid and it certainly wasn't my fault. I mean, obviously I manipulated her. It was fun. But Jane, what I like about you the most is that you really couldn't be manipulated like that. You are more my partner in crime. How funny would it be to do things like that to women together? You and I? I mean, look at Rita over there. I used to say the same type of thing to her."

"Jimmy… she laps it up. Jane soon tells me she loves me. It is pretty apparent to her that no one has ever understood her like me before. She buys a fucking plane ticket from Australia to meet me in Boston. So I fuck her. She flew to Boston to have me buy her a bunch of drinks and then fuck her from behind in her 300 dollar hotel room. I kind of had to fuck her at that point, didn't I? It was much safer that way. By the way, how many times have I done that? I don't even know. How many times have I fucked someone just to back up all the shit I said? That is the worst, Joey. You can't even fucking imagine."

"Shortly thereafter I pull the same scene. I bail on Jane. It usually takes about a month before they really get it."

"So then on to Carrie. Who I meet while playing an online game. Carrie professes to be a lesbian. Even when she starts telling me that she loves me, she still professes to be a lesbian. The thing is no one has ever understood her before like I do."

"She is calling me all night and mooning over me. Same exact thing as always. I try to swear it off, I really do. I know it isn't healthy. Also, it's like having a job. I know I'm making it sound easy but it isn't. It takes an enormous amount of work to get someone to fall in love with you over the internet. For real. It's like a 20 hour a week job to get someone to fall in love with you that doesn't know you."

I was growing impatient. It was becoming a form of misery just to listen to him. It was somehow disturbing to think that there were no laws against this sort of thing. "So why do it?" I said.

He looked at me, confused. "What?"

"If it takes all this time, and it's such a big pain in the ass, and all you're really doing is hurting people, why do it?"

"Jimmy, I'm going to pretend you didn't say that. Now where was I?"

"Carrie," I said.

"Ah, right. With Carrie it goes sort of the same except she is also very into phone sex. With a dude. Even though she is gay. In some ways she was the funniest of all. She was so surprised by what was happening to her."

I couldn't tell what was going on anymore. I couldn't tell if this was some of the strangest bragging I had ever heard, or if he wanted me to tell him he was a piece of shit. I couldn't tell if he really thought anyone wanted to read this in a book. I couldn't tell what he wanted. What the fuck did he want?

"Joey, pay attention, I'm still rolling here. Then it was Katrina, who may have been the easiest. I met her on Facebook. I had taken to just friending random women who I saw on Facebook, and then starting up a conversation by emailing them and saying that I thought the person was someone else, and so sorry but let's still be friends. Katrina not only said that she loved me but I also got her to start talking to me like a dog. She would bark into the phone. It took about three weeks for this to happen. She would write shit like 'Arf' all the time."

"She lived close by. One day I let her come over and suck my dick. Afterwards, she wrote me this."

He had a piece of paper on the couch next to him. Whatever it said, he was proud enough of it to print it out. He shook the page like he was about to give a speech.

"Hang on. Let me read this to you:"

. . .

I like everything about you. I like how you consume my mind when I wake up and before I go to bed. I like how everything just flows with you like air (my favorite element - thank god it's not earth, right?)

I like how you consume me. I like how I am willing to humiliate myself for you when that's what I should be avoiding. I like how I ensnare you with my ridiculousness. I like the subtlety. I like how I can communicate with you by the sounds of the words, not just their inherent meaning. I like how this is a game and not a game at all. I like how you are unique even though that is a ridiculous thing to say about a person and I like that the reason you are so unique to me is because of all the things we have in common.

I like that when you want me to be a coat rack or a shoe horn or a lamp shade that just makes me want to fuck you. And I like that I have no idea when I'm going to do that but that when I do I know you'll be able to kick your feet up on me like an ottoman and that somehow that is irresistible to me because it's fucking stupid.

I love the way I met you. I love remembering the way this all has felt. I love the fact that you've made me feel alive again and safe by talking to me like a shit pile and I love the fact that I do all of this because I categorically do not want to lose you. I love the fact that if that wasn't the exact way to use that word in a sentence you're going to get it anyways because you get words different and you know that incorporating them out of step is how you make them beautiful. I love that I get to suck your cock again this weekend.

I love the fact that I'm addicted to you the same way I am to amphetamines in that it's all psychosomatic except I don't want to quit you and there's no tolerance involved. Except of course that isn't true because I'm always wanting you more.

I love the fact that I got drunk on cheap wine before I wrote this to you. I like that I drink a lot more cheap wine these days than I used to for a while.

So you tell me master... When would you like me to arrive this weekend?

113

What would you like me to do? Who would you like me to be? Shall we spend some time together or should we just meet, greet and shoo...

I will be away the following weekend. So decide how much dumb dog you would like in your life for the time being and I will accommodate you the best this dumb dog knows how.

arf! I love you.

-dog.

. . .

Dylan looked at me over the page.

"I barely knew this woman," he said. "I met her in person that one time, when all she did was suck my dick. You see what I mean? This isn't just me. It isn't. Chicks dig this shit. If I'm insane, they're as crazy as I am."

My mind was numb. I had only been here a couple days but it seemed like I had been here a year. Dylan telling me stories of depravity, Rita frozen in some humiliating position, Staci desperately trying to please. What had started as something that was odd, but at least intriguing had already turned into something that was darker than anything I had encountered. I was supposed to be an observer – the ghostwriter, someone who took it all down without comment. A blank slate. An empty vessel. But I couldn't do it anymore.

I shut off the tape recorder. "Look, I have to say something. What am I going to do with all of this? How am I going to weave this tale of how much you hate women into a story of how you raped God on a vision quest? They don't even do vision quests in Samoa."

He stopped, and all of a sudden he seemed sad. "Oh, they don't? Tell that to Afasa and the other guys at the barbeque business. Also, like I said before, I'm not sure I would call it rape. I think it was more of a consensual thing. I mean, I didn't ask, and He did say no, but..."

"Well, call it what you like," I said.

He shook his head. "You really don't get it, do you? First of all I don't tell people what I do very often. I've gone to counseling, but even then I usually don't open up. Sometimes I have though. Sometimes I've gotten really sad and freaked out about the things that I do. And when I do open up, people ask why I hate women. Just like you did. 'Why do you hate women so much?' But I don't think I do. I really don't. My mom is cool. I like my sister. I was lonely as a kid and I never had a girlfriend, but I don't think I hate women."

"This is the first time, these past couple of days, that I was ever really completely honest with someone about what I have done. And it was you. You got the privilege. I did more than just open up – I was *honest*. And now you're all like, 'Wow this dickbag hates women.' But I don't and I should give you a Colombian necktie for even thinking that. In fact, I love women. I'll bet I love them more than you do."

He paused, took a deep toke on his dope pipe. "Listen, I brought you here to tell you my stories. All my life I've felt judged. I even felt judged in rehab. So I'm paying you to sit there and do your job – without feelings, without passion, without judgment. It was going good for a while, but now I feel like you're starting to judge me, too. And it's judgment that defeats us, Dilly."

"You're right," I said. "I'm starting to judge you. What else am I supposed to do? You think this is a book? It's just a bunch of stories about horrible things you have done. You brought me out here with some tale of a vision quest and an encounter with the gods, and all I'm getting is what a fucking liar you are, and how you like to manipulate and prey on weak-minded women. I don't think you've seen the gods, or fucked God, or anything like that. I think it's just a story you tell yourself because you don't want to admit what a pathetic scene you've got going. You want to pretend this is more than what it is."

Dylan looked thoughtful. "And what do you think it is? This scene of mine?"

I shook my head. "Not much. A waste of life. A waste of three lives. At the moment, it's a waste of four lives, including mine. But I'm out. I can't do this shit anymore."

He nodded. "Okay, Brian. Okay. You want to go see the gods? Is that it?"

"Sure," I said. "That's what I want. That's what I came here for."

"Then we'll go right now," he said. "Just to appease you, we'll go to the fucking mountaintop and we'll see the gods. Will that make you feel better, you fucking ingrate? You ghost-writing, porn star-drugging, Paypal sucking ingrate? You cheated on your girlfriend, you know that? Basically because I paid you five thousand dollars and gave you a slave and told you to."

"Yeah," I said. "I know."

"But you're still better than me somehow, right?"

I shrugged. I didn't say a word.

"Okay," he said. "Ready, fuckstick? Fuck the book. We'll go right now. You catching this, girls? Joey doesn't want to hear my stories anymore. So we're going to see the gods. Come on, Staci. Rita you stay here."

I glanced out the window. The sun was just starting to set. Night was coming on.

"I'll tell you something right now," Dylan said. "This is serious shit you're playing with. It's not a joke. God doesn't just give up the poon to any loser that stops by. If you want to fuck God the way I fucked God, you'd better be ready to die in the attempt."

CHAPTER SIXTEEN

I didn't realize how fucked up I was until I went outside. Since I left Portland I had been doing almost nothing but drinking and smoking weed. How many days had I been there? I no longer remembered.

Dylan was even more wasted than I was. I never saw him sleep the whole time. It was like all he did was sit in the living room, get fucked up, talk, and do things to Rita.

He was waiting for me outside the door. Staci stood next to him. She was naked, except for a pair of red Converse All-Stars on her feet. There was a leash around her neck. Rita was still in the house, naked and blank eyed.

Dylan looked at me, his eyes blood-shot and wild. "Let's go man, we gotta go see the gods. We gotta do this so you don't have to sit here and listen to me talk anymore, right? Let's go. I am totally ready."

Nothing was odd to me anymore. I suppose I could have said no. I suppose I could have just stayed the night, and flown home the next day. But I followed him instead. This was, after all, what I had come here for.

He started to walk. Staci followed behind on the leash. I watched her ass move around as she walked. I didn't want to be turned on right now, I really didn't, but suddenly I was hard as a rock.

We climbed up a steep, narrow trail. The hillside was lush and green, and the cliff dropped away to our left. The water was dazzling in the last of the sunlight. The ocean was a long way down.

Dylan yelled to me over his shoulder.

"You aren't a dick, Joey. You're a fucking ghostwriter. I knew what you were when I hired you. You're a guy that makes money off a guy like me. You don't have good stories, so you steal mine. You hurt my feelings, though. This is the way I am. No one has ever gotten that except for Rita and Staci. They're the only ones that want me for who I am. I guess they're the only ones that really love me."

The wind was picking up as we walked. I could smell the ocean. I had a few women that loved me for who I was, although I didn't recognize that at the time. I loved someone for who she was too, even right now, although I couldn't see her. I couldn't see her because I let myself get dark, I couldn't see her because I lived with someone else, I couldn't see her because I was in Samoa with Dylan fucking Porter walking up a path next to the ocean, staring at some slave girl's naked ass.

After a long while, we stopped walking. I was breathing a little heavily, and there was a sheen of sweat on my face and under my clothes. We were on a stone platform at the top of a cliff, overlooking the water. The sun was going down, but its remnants still burnt the sky. As I watched, it dropped beneath the ocean in a fiery blaze of orange.

Staci looked down at the ground like she was ashamed. Dylan looked me in the eyes and spoke. "It's like a joke to you. It's like a joke to everyone really. I am me. I am doing my thing. I don't care what people think about it. That's why I'm here. I'm here with people that like me for who I am. The rest of you can get fucked. My parents, my exes, all the people I hurt, can get fucked. I met the Gods. They spoke to me."

"They spoke to you?" I said. I put the disdain in my voice. I wanted him to feel it. "I thought you said you gave them a rusty trombone, punched their starfish, got to 5th base…"

He held up his hand. "You'll see what goes down. We're almost ready. The thing is, we don't have the right drugs to do a proper vision quest. I could swing over to Afasa's place, but he has kids, and last time I went there at night he punched me in the stomach. He isn't anyone to fuck with. He cut off a guy's nose once. I saw it. You ever hear of don't bring a knife to a gun fight? Fuck that. Don't bring a nose to a knife fight. Anyway, if we want to fuck God again, we need to transmit ourselves to Him. We need to transcend."

He handed me the leash with Staci at the end of it. "You can

have the girls, Dilly. Treat them like shit. That's what they prefer."
He stepped to the edge of the cliff and stretched out his arms, like he
was getting ready to fly.

He faced out over the ocean, his back to me and Staci. I held
her leash, but it was slack. Her face was very close to mine.

He spoke to me over his shoulder. "The girls are my gift to you.
Or, if you have the strength, you can join me on the immortal plane."

"Dylan..." I said.

He was very close to the edge – really way too close. My heart
started pounding in my chest. After all this, we go to a cliff and the
idiot throws himself off? He was freaking me out. Fuck this guy,
fuck this guy. Seriously. Fuck this guy.

Then all of a sudden, it hit me.

"You won't do it. You've been full of shit the whole time.
There aren't any gods. It is just you. It's just you, and you're here
with these two crazy chicks and you needed me to come out here and
validate you somehow, to validate this life you lead. You aren't
paying me to write, you're paying me to tell you this shit is okay."

Dylan sighed and his body sagged. He stood silent for a long
moment. Then he turned around, and he smiled at me. For the first
time, he looked relaxed.

He shrugged. "You're right. Who am I kidding? I'm not going
to jump off this cliff. Sorry Jimmy, you're right. You are right about
everything."

Staci walked up to him then and pushed him in the chest. Not
violently. She pushed him the way you might give someone you

cared about a joking shove, just to be playful. She wasn't being playful, though.

Dylan wind-milled his arms for just a second, then disappeared over the side. The look on his face before he went was etched upon my mind, the way a flashbulb popping in the dark gets etched upon your eyes. The look was surprise.

For a few seconds, I didn't move. I just stared at the spot where Dylan used to be. I crept to the edge, half thinking that he had dropped to a ledge four feet below, and when I poked my head over, he was going to jump out at me and yell:

"Boo!"

It didn't happen. He was maybe four or five stories below us, his body wedged into some rocks. It looked like his skull had smashed open like an egg. As I watched, a wave washed over him. In the last of the dying light, the pale blue ocean water turned red with his blood. His body moved in the water like seaweed. In the sense that seaweed is limp, like overcooked spaghetti. There are no bones in seaweed.

"Oh, man," I said.

Staci was beside me then. "He never made a sound," she said.

"What?"

"He fell all that way. He didn't scream, cry out. Nothing."

I looked at Staci. I guess I should have felt something but I didn't. It didn't matter. Dylan dead on the rocks didn't mean anything more to me than Rita frozen back in the house. I was on a cliff. I was holding a leash and Staci was naked next to me. I guess I should have held it tighter.

"He's dead," I said to her.

She nodded. "Yeah. I think he must be. Sure looks that way."

"What are we going to do?"

She looked at me. "About what?"

"I don't know. The cops? Long prison sentences in a strange country?"

"Oh. That." She shrugged. "Everybody around here knows he's crazy. They all know he's drunk and on drugs every day. Maybe he killed himself. Maybe he just slipped and fell off."

I grabbed her by her shoulders. She raised her head and looked me in the eyes. I shook her, but actually not too hard.

"Staci. Why did you do that? What the fuck were you thinking?"

She didn't speak for a moment. Then she quietly said, "He didn't really know me at all. And I didn't really love him. I haven't even liked him for a long time. He wasn't a very nice person."

I looked out at the darkening sky. Here and there, the lights of moored sailboats dotted the water.

"Then why did you stay here?"

"I'm a slave. I have a master, and he uses me for sex, or whatever he likes. This is what I do."

"What will you do now?"

She stepped closer to me. Our bodies were just inches apart. Our faces came closer. "I guess I'll be looking for a new master."

They gave us a little bit of shit at customs about the leash. But not as much as you might expect. And we did hit the traditional Samoan barbecue before we left the island. Dylan was right about that. It was really, really good.

The End

ABOUT THE AUTHOR

Brian Whitney has been called "America's favorite sex addict." He has been a counselor, a landscaper, and a case worker at a homeless shelter. His interests include ruminating, perseverating and hanging out in bad places. If you have a Great Dane he will like you immediately.

He writes mostly about sex addiction, from the perspective of someone who has been very, very addicted to sex. Don't worry – he's almost better now. His writing has appeared in the Huffington Post, Business Insider, Substance.com, TheFix.com, and many other places.

In addition to Raping the Gods, he is the author of 37 Stories About 37 Women and Am I Pleasing You? He is also the co-author of memoirs with legendary porn stars Porsche Lynn and Rebecca Lord. His website is www.brianwhitney-writing.com.